'You want to
murmured, j

'No...of course not. I appreciate your
company...very much.' Elaine found herself
chattering quickly, to prevent any silences that she
knew would be voids between them—voids that
would be filled with a rush of sexual need so strong
that they would be swept along with it. And she
didn't want that. She wasn't ready for a man like
Raoul Kenton...not yet.

Rebecca Lang trained to be a State Registered Nurse in Kent, England, where she was born. Her main focus of interest became operating theatrework, and she gained extensive experience in all types of surgery on both sides of the Atlantic. Now living in Toronto, Canada, she is married to a Canadian pathologist, and has three children. When not writing, Rebecca enjoys gardening, reading, theatre, exploring new places, and anything to do with the study of people.

THE HEALING TOUCH

BY
REBECCA LANG

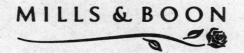

MILLS & BOON

*MILLS & BOON, the Rose Device and
LOVE ON CALL are trademarks of the publisher.
Harlequin Mills & Boon Limited,
Eton House, 18-24 Paradise Road, Richmond, Surrey TW9 1SR*

© Rebecca Lang 1996

ISBN 0 263 79860 7

*Set in Times 10 on 11 pt. by
Rowland Phototypesetting Limited
Bury St Edmunds, Suffolk*

03-9611-52378

Made and printed in Great Britain

CHAPTER ONE

'WAIT a moment. . .don't put that on yet. Who have I got here?'

Elaine Stewart, R. N., hesitated as she stood on tiptoe reaching for a disposable face mask from the box that was on a shelf above the row of scrub sinks outside Unit 2 in the vast operating theatres of University Hospital, Gresham, Ontario, where she worked.

The masculine voice had spoken just behind her, a voice that she recognised as belonging to Dr Raoul Kenton, even though she had not heard his approach. He was definitely early for the operation. No doubt he had been in the hospital all evening and had not been able to go home after the day of operating. Now here they were, about to start work again, with no real break to speak of.

'Hold it!' A warm hand covered hers for a few seconds as the mask was plucked from her grasp. Slowly she straightened up and turned round.

She had been just about to put on the face mask and start to wash her hands and arms for the required number of minutes prior to putting on a sterile gown and a pair of latex gloves. It was eight o'clock in the evening and the operating rooms were very quiet after the mad rush of the day shift and the early evening. From a main corridor outside she could hear the sound of someone being paged on the hospital intercom, emphasising their isolation in their own unit.

'Oh. . .' Startled, Elaine turned to look at her medical colleague. During the brief time in which their eyes met she was aware that Dr Kenton was appraising her in that unconscious masculine way that surgeons had in a work context when they were looking at nurses, where the unspoken rule was look but don't touch.

And 'look' he sure did! Elaine thought a little wildly, trying to subvert the pull his attraction had on her. In a few seconds his eyes moved from her face over her trim body in the pale blue one-piece scrub suit and back to her face. Her hair was covered with one of those unflattering blue tissue paper caps with the elasticated edging and she put her hands up to it self-consciously, pulling it down over her ears.

'Ah. . .it's you,' he said, 'Little Miss Stewart. . . Elaine, isn't it?'

'Yes. . .' she said, annoyed with herself because her voice had come out in a breathy whisper. She cleared her throat. 'Yes, that's right,' she added more firmly. 'I'm not sure about the "little".'

'You *are* little,' he smiled.

'Compared with you, I guess I am,' she answered lightly, trying to be cool, yet suddenly very aware—as her eyes made visual contact with his again—that from a personal point of view working with Raoul Kenton was going to be. . .well. . .difficult. There was something about him—several things about him, in fact— that unnerved her.

He was attractive in a rather unusual way. Instead of 'tall, dark, and handsome' he was tall, broad, fair. . . and very, very attractive.

'You're the one scrubbing for me with this liver case, I guess. . .little Miss Stewart?'

'Looks like it, doesn't it?' she said cheekily, grinning slightly, too tired and too keyed up to go into an adoring nurse routine for him. Not that she thought he expected it, or that she would do it. No. . . Raoul Kenton seemed to have his feet planted too firmly on the ground for that. Unlike some she could mention—and preferred not to think about now.

'Mmm. That's great,' he said, his voice a casual, deep drawl. A slight smile quirked his mouth. 'This is your first liver transplant, I understand? Welcome to the team.'

The smile he gave her then, starting with a warmth in his eyes, made her heart turn over and she found herself smiling back naturally in spite of an attempt at reticence. It wouldn't do to get too attracted to Raoul Kenton. As far as she knew, which wasn't much, he was otherwise engaged. Her curiosity about him was growing, particularly as they were to be thrown together in the hot-house atmosphere of the transplant scene. She would have to ask Angie Clark, who seemed to know what was going on. . .

He had thick, naturally blond hair that was sun-bleached. As she stood close to him now and looked at his uncovered hair she could see that the blond was liberally interspersed with silver-grey at the temples and on the top of his head. The hair was longish, giving him a slightly rakish air. It was certainly too long for a surgeon.

'Thank you,' she said, a little belatedly, 'I'm glad to be on the team. Yes, it is my first liver transplant.' She spoke evenly, brightly, hoping that he would not sense the tension in her. 'I've just spent two years on the kidney transplant team, though. From what I hear about the liver team, the kidney service is much, much busier.'

'Yes, that's true,' he conceded, seeming very relaxed himself and willing to take time with her. 'There are more complications with livers. . .and of course the kidneys can come from live donors, whereas we have to wait for someone to die in an accident or some such, as you know, before we can get a donor liver. It's a whole new ball game.'

Unlike most fair individuals he did not have blue eyes. His were an unusual tawny brown, set in a face of craggy, sensual features...a straight nose, a firm, well-cut mouth. His skin bore the marks of a light summer tan and had the slightly roughened texture of someone who enjoyed being in the country when time permitted. Definitely an unusual-looking man, she thought...very masculine and attractive to women and yet one who did not seem ready to capitalise on that fact.

'Could I have that mask now, please, Dr Kenton?' Elaine said, holding out her hand. 'I have to get scrubbed for the case.'

'Sure,' he said, handing her back the disposable paper mask and then watching her as she tied it in place over her nose and mouth and topped it off with plastic goggles which she took from her pocket.

He backed up against a sink, leaning with his arms behind him on the edge of it, supporting his weight so that the V-necked green cotton scrub suit top that he wore was pulled tautly across his broad chest, drawing her eyes. 'It's not easy to be on call for this team,' he said, the deep timbre of his voice rich with a rare empathy. 'To come back here with the knowledge that you will have to work for the greater part of the night, having already put in a full day's work.'

'Well, I'm used to it now. Used to being exhausted most of the time,' she laughed lightly, not wanting him to guess how close to the bone his remarks were and just how exhausted she really was. 'It isn't any different for you.'

How could he seem so casual; she wondered, when she herself was so churned up inside? In spite of her confident assertion she *was* nervous because this was her first on-call for the liver transplant team, her first time to scrub for an operation that was more complex, more time-consuming, than a kidney transplant. Maybe her feelings were not obvious to him or any observer, any more than his were readily available to her.

'I guess we can say that we already know each other pretty well, Miss Stewart, since you scrubbed for me earlier for that abdominal perineal resection,' he said, smiling at her slightly, 'as well as those other cases over the past two months.'

'Yes. . . But, as you say, this is a whole new ball game,' she said brightly, 'which I would not have got into if I thought I couldn't cope.'

'I'm sure,' he said. It seemed that he didn't quite know what to make of her. In the two months that they had been working together they had not had an opportunity to exchange many words other than over purely work-related matters.

Elaine recalled their afternoon session. One of their patients had had a cancerous tumour of the rectum which Dr Kenton had removed, giving the patient a colostomy—an opening of the bowel directly onto the abdominal wall. 'I really enjoy scrubbing for those abdominal-perineal resections,' she said enthusiastically, aware that he was watching her closely as she turned on the taps at the sink. 'I guess because it's a life-saving operation for the patient, even though the end result may take a while for them to accept. . .'

'Mmm. . .I thought you enjoyed the challenge of it,' he murmured. 'I also thought you were an excellent scrub nurse.'

'Thank you. . . And, from the scrub nurse's point of view, it's something to really come to grips with.' Elaine flushed slightly at his unexpected praise, aware that her enthusiasm for general abdominal surgery was running away with her and that he, as a sophisticated man and surgeon, might think her a little naïve and even gauche. There was a certain light of amusement on his face.

'Well, I must get scrubbed,' she said briskly,

adjusting her plastic goggles and reaching up to the shelf for one of the sterile scrub brushes from a box there. For some reason she found that her eyes kept straying back to Dr Kenton.

'Do I pass?' Raoul Kenton said softly, unexpectedly, his eyes amused, when a few moments of silence had ensued. Those eyes showed intelligence, humour, empathy. . .and something else that she could not at the moment define when she looked at him in startled incomprehension. There was a certain quality of something like sadness in him, too; a deep knowledge that she could find no words for.

'What. . .what do you mean?' she said.

'Your eyes were going over me just then like I was a suit of clothes you were thinking about buying in a store,' he said. 'So. . .do I pass?'

'I. . . Yes.' The image he had conjured up made her smile, bringing a lightness to her that she so needed at that moment, and she resisted an urge to giggle. At the same time she found herself slowly blushing as she lowered her eyes. 'I'm sorry. . .I didn't mean to stare. It's just that I usually see you with a cap, a mask, a gown and goggles. It's rather like being in purdah most of the time.'

'Yeah. . .' he said.

'Even though I haven't scrubbed for a liver transplant before,' she said hurriedly, 'I *am* very familiar with all the instruments, of course, and I've observed a few of the operations. . . Jill Parkes saw to that. I've had a lot of experience with abdominal surgery. Angie Clark will be scrubbing with me to look after the sutures.'

He was looking at her astutely. 'If you do as well as you did earlier today you'll be great,' he said. 'Maybe I should just go over a few things with you now. I know you want to get scrubbed. . .I won't take long. Make a start.'

As he spoke he reached up to the shelf to get one of the caps that the surgeons wore. It was one that covered his head, face and neck, just leaving his eyes, nose and mouth uncovered. She watched as he put it on. Later he would put on a mask over his nose and mouth as well. In the actual operating room they always wore the plastic goggles to guard their eyes against splashes of blood, from which they could possibly get hepatitis or the deadly HIV.

'The woman we're operating on tonight has cryptogenic cirrhosis,' he explained to her while she began the scrub process, running warm water over her hands and arms and working up a lather with the antiseptic solution, not losing her awareness of him for one moment. She nodded.

'That's a fancy term for saying that the origin of her liver disease is unknown. She's been waiting at home for several weeks for this operation—waiting for the call to come in. These patients with chronic liver disease have a lot of scarring and adhesions of the liver. Getting the diseased liver out is often the most time-consuming and difficult part of the operation.'

'So I understand,' Elaine murmured, scrubbing busily.

He changed his position, lounging with ease against the scrub sink as he looked at her. She wished he wouldn't do that. 'Putting in the donor liver is a cinch in comparison,' he explained. 'As you know, they have a lot of blood-clotting problems which cause great difficulties for us in the OR because they bleed at the slightest trauma so we have to proceed very, very carefully while we're dissecting out the diseased liver.'

'Yes, I see,' she murmured, hoping that he didn't think she was a complete idiot. Yet he was not being patronising; he was just filling her in, taking the trouble to communicate before the fact, which she appreciated.

'From your point of view, as the scrub nurse, I'll need lots of small sponges with which to do the dissecting. . .I use those dental pledgets, cut in half and mounted on the long, curved Kocher clamps. . .and the long, fine, blunt-tipped scissors, plus the cautery. We won't actually clamp off any major arteries or veins in the liver until all the other tissue has been freed from the liver bed. . .and the donor liver is right there on the table, ready for us.'

'I see,' Elaine said, nodding.

For a few more minutes he continued to talk to her, while she murmured understanding, until Angie Clark, her co-scrub nurse, burst through the door of Unit 2 to join them at the scrub sinks.

'Hi!' Angie said, breathlessly, 'What's this? A lecture? You should have called me, Elaine. I'd like to be in on it.' It was very evident that Dr Kenton was a favourite of hers.

'He. . .he's just going over the basics—things that you know already.' Elaine said. She turned to Raoul Kenton. 'Thanks, Dr Kenton. I'll be OK.'

'I'm sure you will,' he smiled at them both. 'See you in there.'

As he walked away from them down the corridor Angie watched him go until he was out of earshot, busying herself with tucking a few errant strands of her frizzy ginger hair under her operating cap.

'You know,' Angie said, beginning the scrub process also, 'there's something about that guy that turns my innards to jelly. Those eyes. . .like tiger eyes! And the way he moves! Mmm!' She gave a long murmur of appreciation. 'A pity about his wife and kid, wasn't it? What a tragedy for anyone to have to live with. I'd go stark, raving mad if it had happened to me.'

'Wife and kid? I don't know anything about his private life, Angie. . . And not much about his professional life, come to that,' Elaine said, feeling a frisson of shock and an odd regret that Raoul Kenton had been...or was...married.

'Is he married now?' she asked, even though there was a strange reluctance in her, vying with her curiosity, to know anything about a wife or a child. 'And what tragedy?'

'He isn't married now...as far as I know,' Angie said as she lathered her arms generously. 'I heard that his child died...the one and only.'

Elaine drew in her breath sharply on a sigh. 'Tell me about it some time, Angie. I'm curious. I guess it would be surprising if he hadn't been married. He...he *is* rather gorgeous. I agree with you there.'

'It was five years ago that it happened but, if you ask me, it's still affecting him. You can tell sometimes; there's something about him. They say he hasn't been interested in a woman since then.' Angie lowered her voice. 'Not what you'd call really...*interested*. You know! I don't suppose he's cried off sex *all* that time... a guy like him...but that isn't the same thing, is it? What he's got going with Dr Della Couts I can't imagine! She's so sort of...unreal. One of those plastic women, like a Barbie doll!'

'Oh, come on, Angie! You're just jealous.' Elaine laughed, giving her hands and arms a final rinse under the running water and trying to stifle her curiosity and a continued odd feeling of something like foreboding. She did not want to think right now of the charismatic Dr Kenton as having had something unhappy in his background.

'You'd better believe it!' Angie agreed amiably. 'Wouldn't you just like to get your hands on him yourself?'

Elaine grinned at Angie briefly, refusing to be drawn completely. 'Oh, sure! Who wouldn't? But I don't know anything about him,' she repeated slowly, certain that this was not the time or the place to talk about it either. If there was a mystery, a tragedy, in Dr Kenton's life she didn't really want to know any more about it now.

'I'll put you in the picture some time,' Angie promised meaningfully. 'What would we do in this place without the gossip, eh? Life wouldn't be worth living!'

'I won't have any trouble keeping awake for this—I couldn't sleep if I tried,' Elaine said, deliberately changing the subject. 'My heart's beating like a tom-tom.'

'That's because you've just been talking to Raoul Kenton,' Angie laughed.

'Maybe. I just wish my first liver transplant could have been scheduled during the day,' she said feelingly.

'Yeah. . .I thought you could do the instruments and I'd do the sutures, if that's OK with you. Then maybe next time we'll switch around,' Angie said. 'All those instruments will be familiar to you. . .all those long clamps and other stuff. Then I could teach you the sutures in sequence as we go along.'

'Sure. That's great, Angie.' She liked Angie, whose bubbly, chatty exterior hid a very sensitive interior. She was bright, good at her job, loyal and helpful with her colleagues, while her unruly ginger-coloured hair, a mass of curls, seemed to complement her personality perfectly. Elaine wondered briefly whether her own light brown hair with its bronze highlights and her large grey eyes complemented her personality. Sometimes, these days, she wasn't sure herself who she was or what she was. . . Sometimes all she knew was that she was very, very tired.

Jill Parkes, the unit head nurse, opened the door from their designated operating room to see what progress they were making.

'Get a move on, you guys,' Jill chivvied them good-naturedly, 'otherwise we'll have those surgeons breathing down our necks before we're completely ready. You know how gung-ho those guys are! The donor should be here any minute.'

Inside the operating room Elaine dried herself with a sterile towel and put on her sterile gown and latex gloves. Cathy Stravinsky, the other RN who was a second 'circulating nurse' with Jill, moved up behind her to fasten her gown at the back. 'Hi, Elaine,' she said, working quickly. 'I've given you everything you could possibly need for now. I'll count the sponges and instruments with you as soon as you're ready.'

'Thanks, Cathy.' Elaine quickly made a mental note of all the instruments they would count, as well as needles, sponges, small towels and everything else that could possibly be left by mistake inside the patient's abdominal cavity. Then, at the end of the operation before the abdominal cavity was finally sewn up, they would count everything again at least twice. It was a tedious but necessary task.

A calmness came over Elaine as she approached the large stainless-steel table on which a bulky sterile pack had been opened up ready for her, together with her trays of instruments. Now she was in her element; from here on she was the expert, knowing exactly what to do. In this room there would be no unnecessary interruptions; a kind of concentrated peace would reign. She would be OK.

Dr Claude Moreau, the staff anaesthetist, came in when Elaine and Angie were well on the way to having their sterile set-up ready.

'Hi, *mes filles*,' Dr Moreau greeted them good-humouredly. 'Here we go again, eh?' He was a tall, dark, French-Canadian, who loved to tease. 'I shall want to bring the patient in here in about ten minutes. Is that OK with you guys? I'm putting in another IV line out there in the corridor.' He proceeded to check his anaesthetic machine and the other equipment that he would be using.

'That's fine with us, Dr Moreau,' Elaine smiled at him. Dr Moreau elicited a certain amount of awe; it was the anaesthetist, after all, who kept the patient alive as well as asleep, who monitored and balanced the delicate body chemistry of the anaesthetised patient and who gave the blood transfusions and intravenous drugs.

'I think he's great!' Angie echoed Elaine's thoughts when Dr Moreau had gone out. 'I'd put myself in his hands any day. The surgeon, by comparison, is a mere technician, I always think. Now, Elaine. . .take a peek at these sutures I've got ready. They're all lined up in the order that Dr Kenton will use them. He doesn't vary from that unless something out of the ordinary happens. . .and I've got spares for that.'

'OK.'

Dr Matt Ferrera, the senior surgical resident, came in later with his hands and arms wet from the scrub sinks, closely followed by Tony Asher, the surgical intern.

'How are you, Elaine?' Matt asked her as she handed him a sterile towel to dry himself. 'I never get to have a proper conversation with you these days.' Matt, who was of Portuguese extraction, was darkly macho and flirtatious.

'Just great, Matt.'

'What's with you and Matt?' Angie whispered afterwards, when the two assistant surgeons were gowned and gloved. Such chatter served as a little light relief in the tense moments of waiting to start. Through a window they could see that Raoul Kenton was scrubbing at the sinks together with a senior colleague, Dr Mike Richardson. Their patient was already anaesthetised on the operating table.

Elaine took a deep, nervous breath. 'Nothing to speak

of,' she said, her eyes darting this way and that over their sterile set-up, making quite sure, for the hundredth time maybe, that nothing was missing.

'You are still going out with him, though?'

'On and off,' she said in an undertone just as Dr Kenton came into the room, his face obscured by the accoutrements of surgery.

'Here's the big guy,' Angie muttered.

'Here we go, kid,' Elaine said. 'Wish me luck!'

'I think we can finally see the wood for the trees, Mike.' Dr Kenton carefully took his gloved hands out of the patient's abdominal cavity and stepped back from the operating table. 'Ah. . . That's better.' He flexed his shoulders, moving them up and down. 'A little more dissection and that's it, I think.'

'Yeah. . .that should do it,' Dr Mike Richardson agreed.

Elaine glanced quickly and surreptitiously at the wall clock, amazed to see that they were already into the early hours of the morning. The diseased liver had not yet been removed. The donor liver had been in the room for some time in sterile plastic bags surrounded by ice.

'The donor liver,' Angie whispered, seeing the direction of her gaze, 'will have been perfused with cooling and nutrient agents by the other surgical team to keep the cells alive. Remember that bit from your orientation?'

'Yes,' Elaine said quietly, thoughtfully. She frowned and blinked tiredly. An individual had died and now their patient on the operating table would get a chance to live. As she glanced at Raoul Kenton's bent head and then at the other surgeons going quietly about their tasks she felt a moment of fierce pride. They were among the best. . .and she was part of the team!

Angie caught her glance and gave her a meaningful grin, knowing exactly what she was feeling.

Surreptitiously Angie gave her the thumbs-up sign and Elaine returned the gesture.

'Is that some sort of sign language you've got going there?' Dr Mike Richardson asked.

'Sure! And it's secret,' Angie said. Suddenly there was a flurry of conversation in the room as the tension momentarily eased.

'Wake up, Dr Asher,' Raoul Kenton's light admonition made everyone laugh as the surgical intern, Tony Asher, who had appeared to be falling asleep on his feet, jerked into a state of greater alertness. 'As you can see——' he looked at both Tony Asher and Elaine '——the liver is now connected only by its major blood vessels and the bile ducts. . . The very last thing we're going to do before we take it out is to cut these blood vessels. You'll notice that all the surrounding tissues have been dissected back so that the vessels can be clearly seen.'

'It's fascinating,' Elaine said. And it was. It never ceased to amaze her that this operation and others like it were possible.

'I'm glad you think so, Miss Stewart,' Raoul Kenton said lightly, 'because this is how you're going to be spending a lot of your nights from now on.'

There was general amusement again. Why then did she feel that there was innuendo in his words— something just for her? Heaven forbid that she was developing a schoolgirl crush on Dr Raoul Kenton. With the others she shared the half-rueful laughter.

'I don't suppose she does much else with her nights,' Matt Ferrera chipped in roguishly.

'You would know, would you, Dr Ferrera?' Mike Richardson asked.

'I have a pretty good idea,' Matt said, giving Elaine a wink as they all paused to take a few moments to consider the next surgical move.

There were four doctors at the operating table. Then

there was the anaesthetist and his senior resident who, between them, had given the anaesthetic to the patient and were monitoring her condition very carefully and precisely with a great deal of state-of-the-art equipment. She was being transfused with blood, plasma and other intravenous fluids.

'Elaine,' Jill addressed her quietly while the surgeons were discussing progress, 'Do you mind if Angie takes a break now? This seems like a good time. Will you be OK on your own for about twenty-five minutes?'

'Yes, I'm pretty well organised,' Elaine whispered back.

'Then you can go for a coffee and snack when Angie gets back,' Jill promised.

'There's nothing I'd like better,' Elaine smiled her relief, 'My bladder's bursting, never mind the need for coffee!' Not to mention her aching feet and eyes that felt as though she had not closed them for a week. There was no need to mention them. The others would be feeling exactly the same way—longing for those first few sips of fresh, hot coffee and the first bite of a sweet doughnut, one of many that the hospital provided for the transplant staff at night. 'How about you, Angie?'

Angie stepped down from the large, flat stool on which she and Elaine had had to stand in order to reach their instruments easily on the high instrument table that was positioned across the patient's body. 'You're so right!' she whispered, grimacing in mock pain. 'I'll be heading straight for the washroom.'

Dr Kenton addressed her again. 'You've done very well, Miss Stewart. What do you say, Mike?' Suddenly all attention was upon Elaine.

'Thank you. Don't speak too soon,' she quipped, feeling her cheeks warming and an inward glow from his welcome praise. It was not every day that a surgeon bothered to compliment his scrub nurse. 'We have a long way to go yet.'

'The worst part is over,' Dr Kenton said, peering at her through his goggles and leaning very close to her as he stood on the opposite side of the operating table. 'Let me explain what we're going to do next. And you pay attention too, Tony—you might learn something.'

Everyone laughed again as Dr Asher jerked to attention and craned forward to look into the abdominal cavity, kept open by a large self-retaining retractor. 'I know exactly what's going on,' he said.

'That's great, Tony. . .although I'm not sure I believe you. Give me a little buzz, please, Elaine. Step on the ''coag'' pedal—I just want to get this little bleeder here,' Dr Kenton said.

'I assume you mean Tony, Raoul,' Mike Richardson said, poker-faced.

'He's not that much of a bleeder,' Dr Kenton remarked, chuckling, while he coagulated the oozing blood vessel with the electo-cautery and Elaine put her foot on the appropriate pedal that was positioned on the floor to activate the electric current, a job that Angie had been doing up to now. The gadget made a satisfying fizzing noise as the vessel was sealed off.

'OK. . .here we go. Give me two of the long arterial clamps, Elaine. Then the long-handled knife. Ready with the suction, Matt?' Raoul Kenton spoke calmly, while Elaine reached for the appropriate clamps that she had ready.

'Yeah, I'm ready,' Matt replied.

'What I'm going to do now is cut these major blood vessels that are holding the liver in place,' Raoul Kenton explained. 'Then all we have to do is lift it out, tidy up the liver-bed somewhat and it's ''all systems go'' for attaching the new liver.'

During the period of intense concentration, when the

major vessels of the diseased liver that connected it to the main blood supply were finally clamped and cut, it was not surprising that Elaine lost all track of time. Watching closely, with the necessary instruments on hand, she became totally absorbed.

It was only when Cathy Stravinsky came into the room, her hands and arms dripping water from having scrubbed, that Elaine had the first intimation that something was wrong. Frowning, she glanced quickly at the clock to discover that Angie had been gone from the room for forty-five minutes. When the liver was finally out, placed in a large stainless-steel bowl, Cathy took over from Elaine. 'Go for your break now, Elaine,' Cathy whispered.

'What's up?' she whispered back.

'Jill will explain.'

Their head nurse's face looked pale and taut as she motioned Elaine out of the room. 'Angie's just discovered that she knows the liver donor. . .a young guy who had a motorbike accident. He was in the intensive care unit. Anyway, she's in a terrible state,' Jill said quickly, resignedly, her faced creased with worry. 'I'm going to send her home by taxi. What an awful thing to happen. . .and when it's your first liver transplant, too. I need Cathy as a circulating nurse so when you've had your coffee break, Elaine, I'm afraid you're on your own.'

CHAPTER TWO

ELAINE stripped off her gloves and soiled surgical gown, feeling sick with shock.

'Oh, my God! What a thing to happen. How often does that happen? One in a thousand? One in a million? Poor Angie. . .where is she?' she asked Jill, her fatigue forgotten.

'She's in the main nursing office. I'm giving her a chance to calm down and then I'm going to call the taxi. There's someone at her place to be with her so she won't be alone for the rest of the night,' Jill explained quickly and tensely in her usual efficient way.

'What. . .what actually happened?'

'When she came out for her coffee-break she checked the donor team's operating chart to see the name of the donor because she had an idea that it might be the guy she knew. He's been in the intensive care unit for a few days. . .motorbike accident. . .like I said.'

They conferred quickly in the empty corridor. 'Look, Elaine,' Jill said, 'I've got to get back in the OR. Don't let Angie go home until I give the say-so. And, Elaine. . .' she grasped Elaine's arm '. . .you go and get yourself a cup of coffee and something to eat. I don't want you passing out on me! That would be all I need! OK?'

'Yes. . . Don't worry.'

'Be back in the OR in twenty-five minutes. . . scrubbed!'

With a shambling run Elaine moved along the corridor towards the main nursing office. The pain was back in her legs. She had stood in more or less one place for hours and her feet felt swollen so that her usually comfortable uniform shoes were tight.

Angie's ravaged face, streaked with tears and garishly pale under the harsh and unflattering fluorescent lighting in the main nursing office, was the first thing that Elaine focussed on as she rushed into the room. 'Angie,' she burst out, holding her arms open, 'what a thing to happen!'

'I can't believe it,' Angie wailed, tears starting afresh as she allowed her friend and colleague to enfold her in a comforting embrace. 'I don't want to believe it. I. . .I used to know him at school. . .I thought he was recovering. I hadn't seen him for two days. Oh, God. . . Elaine.'

'There was nothing anyone could have done for him, Angie,' Elaine said, the tears of empathy starting in her own eyes. 'I remember that young guy. I was in Intensive Care yesterday visiting someone else. . .I saw that he was in a coma. They said. . .they said he was already brain-dead. He didn't know anything about it, Angie.' Elaine stroked her friend's tumbled hair. 'He was out of it.'

'I'm not much good to you now, am I?' Angie said chokingly. 'I've left you in the lurch.'

'Don't you worry about me,' Elaine said as firmly as she could, her voice wobbling, while feeling as though something had struck her a sharp blow. 'Come into the nurses' lounge with me while I get some coffee. I've got to get back in the OR soon. And you're not to leave here until Jill says so.'

'Oh, I couldn't go in there. . . Not with Dr Kenton or Dr Richardson. . .I couldn't let them see me like this,' Angie said agonisedly.

'They won't be there. Only Tony, maybe.'

'I don't mind Tony,' Angie whispered, as she allowed herself to be ushered gently out.

Sure enough, Tony Asher came in to join them when they were sipping hot coffee. 'Hi, Elaine,' he said. 'Mind if I join you for that coffee? I guess Raoul could see I was about dead on my feet. He's good that way. It's sure good to be out of there for a while, away from all that dedicated concentration. What happened to you, Angie?'

'She knows the donor,' Elaine chipped in quickly, 'but she doesn't want to talk about it any more now; she's already said everything. She'll be going home very soon.'

'Wow!' Dr Asher paused for a moment in pouring himself coffee. 'The luck of the draw, eh? I feel for you, Angie, I really do.'

Angie nodded dumbly. Dr Asher was too sensitive to press the point; he simply looked at her in that quiet, empathetic way he had. Elaine watched the silent play of emotion. Tony was going to be a good doctor. . .was a good doctor. He was nearing the end of his intern year, doing his obligatory stint in surgery. There was still a certain boyish enthusiasm in all that he did, not yet overtaken by cynicism which was an occupational hazard—one among many others.

'Ah, I sure needed that!' Tony smiled at them, having downed a large glass of orange juice in several determined gulps before starting on the coffee.

'Mmm. . .' Elaine drank coffee that was good, hot, strong and sweet. Between mouthfuls of it she ate two doughnuts and four chocolate-chip cookies, feeling her energy level rising as she did so. She eased her aching feet out of her shoes.

'That takes care of the stomach,' Tony remarked when he had finished eating voraciously. 'Now for the bladder. Then we'd better get back in there, otherwise we're going to miss the most crucial part. Excuse me.'

'What a thing to happen, eh, Tony?' she said to him

later when they were once again at the scrub sinks.

'Yeah, absolutely bloody,' Tony agreed. 'But that's life in a hospital. You have to be prepared for anything, even that. . .and learn to roll with the punches. She'll be OK by tomorrow.'

Feeling keyed up in the familiar way, yet very calm at the core of her being, Elaine joined Cathy Stravinsky at the instrument table.

'They're getting the donor liver in position,' Cathy said to her quietly. 'Then they'll be connecting the blood vessels. All the sutures are lined up here. Will you be all right on your own?'

Expertly, calmly, Elaine ran her eyes over the sutures that had already been mounted on needle-holders by Cathy. The needles were the fine, curved ones for stitching arteries and veins; the suture material itself was fine, yet very strong. Raoul Kenton looked up at her then, silently acknowledging her return, and her eyes met his for a second. 'Yes, I'll be all right,' she said.

'Steady! Steady!' Dr Claude Moreau, the anaesthetist, instructed the rest of the staff as the patient was prepared to be transferred, via a special lifting device, from the operating table to a bed that had been wheeled into the operating room. 'Let her down gently. Careful of that IV tubing there. And I don't want that catheter to pull out.'

'OK, I'll take care of the catheter and urine bag,' Jill said.

It was all over. With the others Elaine helped to transfer the patient to the bed on which she would be wheeled the short distance along a corridor to the recovery room, where she would stay for several hours before being transferred to the intensive care unit.

'How do you feel, kid?' Cathy whispered to her as they stood side by side, leaning over the operating table as the transfer was made.

'Great!' she whispered back. 'It was a fantastic experience. I feel a bit as though I've been hit by a ten-ton truck but otherwise I'm just great.'

'Steady! She's awake now,' Dr Moreau said, 'even though she may not be able to move because of the muscle relaxants. She can hear us and feel pain.'

'Hang up the IV bags, Tony. . . Here, take them,' Dr Richardson instructed Dr Asher as they all made a last concerted effort as a team to take care of their patient. In moments she would be handed over to others under the continued care of Dr Moreau and his resident.

'We know you're awake, Linda,' Claude Moreau said calmly and soothingly to the patient, bending down so that his head was close to her ear. With one hand he supported the ventilator tube that was still in Linda's mouth, allowing oxygen into her lungs; with the other hand he gently stroked her cheek, a warm, reassuring human touch. 'The operation's finished. Everything's fine. We're going to give you something for pain.'

Watching, Elaine felt the familiar emotional constriction of her throat. This was what made it all worthwhile; this was what it was all for.

Claude Moreau nodded to his resident. 'Put it in slow. . .real slow. . .and watch the monitors,' he said. They all stood quietly while the anaesthetic resident inserted the needle of a hypodermic syringe through a port in the intravenous tubing and began slowly to inject a little morphine into Linda's veins.

All was well. As Linda was wheeled out of the operating room, together with all the attached tubings and bags of fluid, a mood of elation took over those who were left behind. Raoul Kenton and Mike Richardson stripped off their rubber gloves while Cathy untied their surgical gowns for them.

'Wowee!' Matt Ferrera exclaimed, following their example. 'That was quite something! For a few minutes there I thought that liver wasn't going to fit in.' He took off his green cotton operating cap and ran both hands through his flattened hair.

They all began to chatter and smile as the tension drained away—as the excitement engendered by the operation slowly began to subside.

'Thank you all very much,' Raoul Kenton said, looking at each one of them in turn. 'You were a superb team, as always! Thank you, Jill. . . Thank you, Cathy. And, Elaine. . .you were great.' As he spoke to her he placed a hand very briefly on her shoulder and gave it a slight squeeze before turning away. Then in a flurry all the surgeons were gone from the room.

A warm flush of pleasure momentarily blotted out Elaine's fatigue as the imprint of Raoul Kenton's fingers remained on her skin like a caress.

'He was pleased with you, kid,' Jill said, 'and so he ought to be. In the circumstances I think we all did just great. Now, how about a bit of music while we come down to earth and do the clearing up?'

'Yes, please,' Elaine grinned. 'There's nothing like a mountain of dirty instruments to bring you down from a ''high''.'

Jill fiddled with a few knobs on the wall that allowed taped music to flow soothingly into the room. Some surgeons liked to operate to soft music. Not Dr Kenton, though.

'Where's the gin and tonic, then?' Elaine laughed, quite suddenly wildly elated as she prepared to deal with the used instruments.

'You'll have to be content with hospital tea, kid,' Cathy joined. 'Ah, just think of it. . .we can actually sleep for a whole day and a whole night without interruption!'

'You mean like normal?' Jill laughed in mock awe.

'Yeah!' Cathy said.

The operating rooms were a little eerie in those dead hours leading up to dawn, when those who were awake from necessity would rather be sleeping and when one's energy was at its lowest ebb.

These thoughts occupied Elaine's mind briefly as she walked out of the operating suite to go to the nurses' locker room to change to her outdoor clothing. Her steps were slower than they had been on the inward journey and her thoughts turned to Angie.

'Miss Stewart!' An elevator door had opened behind her and she turned round to see Dr Kenton covering the short distance between them. Now he wore a clean scrub suit of light green under a white lab coat. His uncovered face looked as exhausted as she knew her own would appear to him. 'I thought you might like to have a look at our patient in the recovery room before you go home to see first-hand the results of our team effort. The new liver will be working now.'

'Yes,' she agreed. Although they had just been together for hours she felt drawn to him anew.

'Won't keep you long.' He gave her a tired smile. 'As this is your first liver I thought you should see the visible evidence of the difference a healthy liver makes.'

'Will you be here for the rest of the night?' she asked politely, trying to mask her pleasure at his closeness. As she had turned round she had experienced a slight wave of faintness, no doubt owing to lack of food.

'Oh, I'll have to hang around for a while yet. . . Make sure there's no post-op bleeding. Mostly, Claude and Matt will take over now. And Dr Couts, of course.'

They began to walk in another direction towards the recovery room. As she moved Elaine knew that all was not well with her. Dark specks floated before her eyes from top to bottom, like rain, and she felt a coolness come over her—a slight feeling of sickness. Several times in her life she had fainted and now she knew that this was to be another time. . .just when she had wanted to impress Dr Kenton with her stamina and efficiency. If only she could lie down for a few minutes. . .

'Dr Kenton,' she managed to gasp out the words, 'I think I'm going to faint. Can you please. . .?' The dark rain before her eyes increased in density, through which she could just see Raoul Kenton's face turned towards her and his arms outstretched to her. Then all she was aware of was a loud banging inside her head.

'Lie there,' a voice said to her gently. 'Don't try to get up. You're on the floor but don't worry about that.'

Elaine's eyelids fluttered open, then shut again, just long enough for her to see that she was indeed on the floor with Dr Kenton's lab coat bunched up under her head while he was crouched down beside her. A warm hand was on her wrist, feeling her pulse. The banging in her head, which she realised now coincided with the beating of her heart, was gradually receding.

'I'm sorry.' The words came out through stiff lips. 'I guess I need to eat something.'

'Don't you move,' he said gently, bending close to her so that she could discern a faint tangy scent of an after-shave cologne, a welcome scent after the odours of anaesthetic agents and iodine skin-prep solutions. 'I'm going to get you a drink of water. Then I'm taking you home.' From his tone of voice it was a statement of fact that he would be taking her home.

It was good to be lying down, even on the hard floor. In moments he was back, supporting her head and shoulders while she drank water. 'I'm sorry,' she repeated. 'I know you're busy. I can manage.'

'No, you can't,' he contradicted her briskly, 'and

don't apologise again. You're only human, like the rest of us.'

'I was thinking of Angie Clark,' she said.

'Don't think of saying you're sorry again,' he forestalled her, speaking softly. 'I wouldn't want to work with someone who couldn't admit their humanity. . .or couldn't cry.'

'So much for my tough image,' she said ruefully, attempting humour, looking away from him with a touch of embarrassment now that she felt colour returning to her face.

To her surprise he cradled her against his chest, holding her firmly with both his arms. Through the thin cloth of her scrub suit she could feel his body warmth. 'I've told Dr Moreau to page me if I'm needed,' he said. 'Have you got a car at the hospital?'

'I. . . No, I didn't bring my car. It's in for repairs.' . Elaine swallowed hard, feeling herself in a slightly untenable position as she relaxed against her colleague. 'If you're going my way I would appreciate a ride. But don't put yourself out.'

'I wouldn't have offered if I was putting myself out,' he said a little brusquely. 'I'll meet you outside the entrance of the Fraser wing in about. . .twenty minutes?'

'Yes. Thank you.' Vaguely she wondered why he was bothering with her; he must lead a hectic life.

'I think I ought to come in and make you a cup of coffee. I can't go home with a clear conscience until I know you'll be all right.' Dr Kenton said those surprising words to her when he stopped his car outside her front door so that Elaine had an immediate mental image of her cosy, untidy kitchen in her tiny flat, where her breakfast cup and plate still resided on the table. The flat was on the ground floor of a big old house on a quiet residential street where, at this hour, not a creature stirred.

'I should be making you one,' she said. 'You've been very kind. Yes. . .come in.' Not in a million years would she have imagined this scenario. Dr Kenton generally fraternised with cool, sophisticated career women like Dr Della Couts; he did not, she had assumed, invite himself into nurses' kitchens to make them coffee. Well, he would have to take her as he found her and her flat, too.

When she switched on lights in the hall her cat emerged from the sitting-room then ran back out of sight when confronted with a strange man. Elaine went after him and picked him up.

'Come in,' she said self-consciously, hugging the cat as she returned to the hall. 'Please hang your coat up there on that hook. This is Cornelius. Do you. . .do you like cats?'

He was staring at the cat, a slight frown on his face. 'My daughter had a cat,' he said absently, reaching out to touch the cat's head, 'almost exactly like that.'

Angie's earlier words sounded again in Elaine's mind as she raised her eyes to meet his.

'Where is your daughter now?' Something compelled her to utter those words; they were out before she had realised that she wanted to say them and her heart stilled for a second with a new kind of tension.

'She died five years ago. She had cancer of the bone. . .an osteo-sarcoma.' He stated the facts quietly, words that struck a note of awful finality. With the back of one finger he gently stroked the cat's head, standing close to Elaine as she held her pet.

The reply saddened Elaine unbearably and she longed to reach out and touch him. Somehow, instinctively, she knew that he would not want her to say she was sorry; those words sounded trite when you did not know the

person involved. . .and she hardly knew him, let alone
the child. Only the drama of their shared job brought
them together in a bond of sorts, a bond that normally
did not involve their private lives. Having fainted in
front of him, she did not see that it mattered now that
he was forced into revealing something of his private
life; it somehow redressed a balance between them.

'I. . .feel for you,' she said softly, searching for the
right words. 'It's something that I. . .I can't begin to
imagine.' All she knew at that moment was that if such
a thing ever happened to her she would probably go
mad. . .stark, staring mad. . .as Angie had also said.

All at once the small, enclosed space seemed to be
full of electricity, a frisson that seemed to crackle
between them in the silent house where no one else was
awake. Elaine dropped her eyes from his face, concentrating on his hand as it stroked Cornelius. Almost as a
tangible thing she could feel his unresolved grief. . .and
something else. Was that 'something' for her?

His finger moved from the head of the cat to touch
her hand, over the delicate skin on the inner side of
her wrist, before dropping away. Her small gasp of
awareness was her acknowledgement of her deepening
attraction to him. Quickly she took a step back, feeling the
wall behind her.

'How about that coffee?' he said huskily as she
avoided looking at him by placing the purring cat carefully on the floor.

'He likes you,' she said brightly, deflecting attention.

'Cats usually do,' he murmured. 'I wish I could get
nurses to like me with such alacrity. Perhaps that coffee
will help you to relax, Miss Stewart. Am I such an ogre?'

'No. . . Of course not!' She raised a shocked face to
his, meeting his perceptive tawny eyes.

'You shy away from me like a startled fawn,' he said
softly. 'I guess you prefer to deal with surgeons when

they're safely in the operating room. Hmm?'

Forcing herself to hold his gaze, she confronted him bravely, her heart pounding from a new sexual awareness. 'Well, Dr Kenton, I've had no experience with a surgical staff-man outside of one.'

'Perhaps that should be remedied.' He smiled at her crookedly. 'I'll make you that coffee.' Somehow there was more to his words than a simple offer to make coffee; her heart began to beat fast and deeply. She thought she understood about his daughter and his need to flirt with a young woman. . .if that was what he was doing.

'Come into the kitchen,' she invited as she willed the unbearable tension to subside. 'I think I'd like tea. How about you?' Although the question of what had happened to his wife seemed to burn in her brain it was not one that she could utter now.

'The idea was that I'd make you something,' he reminded her, shrugging out of his coat in her small hallway and filling up the space so that she had to squeeze past him.

'It would be quicker if I did it.' She moved ahead of him, putting on more lights.

'You want to get rid of me?' he murmured, just behind her.

'No. . . Of course not. I appreciate your company. . . very much.' Quickly she cleared the table and filled the electric kettle with water, doing everything carefully and deliberately so that she might not drop something in her agitation.

'What can I do, then?'

'Well. . .' It occurred to her that he might be hungry, as she was. 'Would you like something to eat? I've got lots of food,' she said tentatively, not wanting to appear to be the sort of woman who forced a kind of premature intimacy by offering food. 'If you say yes you can cook it yourself if you like. . .for both of us.'

She found herself chattering quickly, to prevent any silences that she knew would be voids between them — voids that would be filled with a rush of sexual need so strong that they would be swept along with it. And she didn't want that. She wasn't ready for a man like Raoul Kenton. . .not yet.

Surprisingly he grinned then, lightening the somewhat strained atmosphere between them. 'Actually, I'm starving. And if you're hinting that I can't cook you're mistaken. I'm pretty good.'

'If you are to prove it,' she said, flinging open the door of the refrigerator to reveal that it was well stocked, 'take your pick. All the necessary utensils are over here.' With another flourish she indicated cupboards opposite, while returning his grin tentatively. 'I'm going to enjoy watching you.'

Without any further prompting from her he took off the jacket that was part of a very suave grey suit and rolled up the sleeves of his shirt while she watched, fascinated. When he reached for an apron that she had hanging on a hook and put it on, she laughed out loud; it bore the logo SUPER CHEF. 'Does that apply?' she said, still having difficulty in believing that this was happening.

'You can decide that later,' he said.

'Use anything you want,' she said, turning away from him to make tea for them both. Her tiredness was being tempered by an oddly delirious warmth.

In the bathroom, between taking mouthfuls of tea, she washed and added a little make-up to her pale, waif-like face. 'I look like a raccoon,' she smiled at herself ruefully, creaming off black smudges of mascara from under her eyes. There was no way that she could ever be like the beautiful magnolia-skinned Della Couts, yet she did have something. The grey eye-shadow that she touched to her upper lids accentuated her large eyes and the haunted, mysterious quality that characterised her features. And she did have a good mouth, full and well shaped, with a definite Cupid's bow. Her high cheek-bones added interest to her heart-shaped face.

As she coloured her mouth subtly with a little lipstick and brushed her gold-tipped light brown hair so that it fluffed out in feminine wisps around her face she wondered whether Raoul Kenton thought she had a nice mouth. . .whether he had any thoughts along those lines in relation to her, in spite of the physical need that she sensed in him. When he had held her in his arms earlier she had wanted him to kiss her. Even in her distress she had been uncommonly aware of his closeness.

'Don't be an idiot,' she whispered, looking fiercely at her reflection. 'He's not for you.'

'I took you at your word,' he said to her when she emerged. 'I've used what I liked. . . Not breakfast. . . more of a brunch.' In her small kitchen he looked very large, very masculine, making her feel correspondingly small, very womanly. It was not often that a man made her feel like that, not even Matt Ferrera.

'Let me see,' she murmured, coming close. 'It certainly smells good.'

He took off the apron and flung it over a chair. With every fibre of her being Elaine was aware of him.

'That looks wonderful,' she said, overcome with a certain shyness. In a very short time Dr Kenton had produced grilled salmon steaks, savoury rice and a tasty sauce made out of mayonnaise, fresh dill and pickled capers, plus a salad with a very nice dressing. 'I didn't suspect you would be a good cook.'

'Why not?' he challenged, giving her a grin that momentarily erased the signs of fatigue on his face. 'I've had a lot of practice at cooking in a hurry. I'm quite good at one or two other things as well, Miss

Stewart.' From the tone of his voice she knew that he was teasing her; that he was deliberately leaving her to draw her own conclusions. From some other man it might have sounded snide. . .but not from him.

They ate the food with French bread and white wine. Music from a radio played softly in the background: Elaine had put it on to fill any awkward silences that might fall between them. It did not work out that way— as she sat opposite him at the small kitchen table she found that the silences were companionable for the most part. The wine speedily relaxed both of them. They talked about houses, about the old neighbourhood in which she lived. . .anything but work. Then he talked to her about the West Indies, where he liked to go for vacations.

'This is nice,' he murmured to her when they had finished eating. 'A dinner at dawn.' He relaxed back in his chair, looking at her through half-closed lids as he held his wine glass in front of him. Some men would undoubtedly have said, 'We should do this again,' some meaning it, some not meaning it. He did not say it.

'Yes,' she agreed, smiling at him somewhat shyly. 'Thank you for your company. . . Dr Kenton.'

'Feeling better now?' He looked at her quizzically as he leaned forward casually on the table.

'A lot better,' she said, standing up, more sensitive to his closeness when they no longer had the distraction of food. 'Would you like some ice-cream? I've got strawberry and chocolate. And coffee?'

'I'll have all three, please.' He followed her movements with his eyes indolently as she prepared to serve ice-cream and make coffee. 'Call me Raoul. You can't go on calling me "Dr Kenton".'

'All right,' she agreed, keeping her back to him so that he could not see the flush that spread over her cheeks, conscious of his scrutiny of the casual sweater and comfortable old jeans that she wore—had worn under her coat for the on-call the night before.

No way was she going to let on that she found him as attractive as did just about every other female in the entire operating suite. Because then he would show her—politely and charmingly, no doubt, as he had with them—that if there was any choosing to be done—a serious relationship to be contemplated—he would be the one to do the choosing. Not that he would be averse to an hour or so in her bed like any normal man, she surmised, if she were to offer herself. . .

As though on a cue his beeper went off when they were halfway through dessert. 'Could I use your telephone?' he asked, standing up. In an instant the professional world, only incompletely in abeyance, intruded once again.

'Yes, of course. It's in the sitting-room.' When he went off to answer the beeper Elaine found herself praying that the call would not be anything to do with trouble for their transplant patient. As she cleared away the remains of their first course she found herself holding her breath for long moments, as though by doing so she could hear what he was saying. She merely looked at him questioningly when he came back.

'You needn't worry. . .' he interpreted her glance '. . .it's just Matt Ferrera, giving me the result of the latest liver-function test on Linda. It's looking good, I'm pleased to say. However, Elaine. . .' he picked up the apron that he had flung over the back of his chair earlier and came towards her '. . .I'm afraid I really must go as soon as I've finished that delicious ice-cream and coffee.' He put the strap of the apron over her head. 'I guess you're thinking that it's just like a man to go off when there's clearing up to do? Hmm?'

'No. . .I don't keep a tally of things like that,' she

said. 'It's too petty. You did cook the meal, after all. It was really great!'

When he smiled down at her, standing very close, she found that all she could do was look up at him, her lips slightly parted, held by the fascination of that melding of an unusual masculine ruggedness and a sophistication that she saw in him. His hands, having placed the strap around her neck, moved down to rest lightly on her shoulders.

The touch had an electrifying effect; she felt her pupils dilate with shock and sexual awareness. When he looked at her mouth she knew that he was going to kiss her. Even though questions formed urgently in her mind. . . Where is your wife?. . . Do you still love her?. . .she knew that she could not prevent her response to him, a response that would be powerful and utterly self-annihilating.

Simultaneously they moved so that she was in his arms; his firm mouth was covering hers, her fragile body overwhelmed by his powerful one as he held her strongly against him. A sharp flare of utter delight held her in thrall as his warmth pervaded her soft lips. There was nowhere for her to put her arms but around his neck.

CHAPTER THREE

A FEW days later the memory of Raoul Kenton's kiss was vivid in her mind, yet at the same time Elaine was having trouble believing that it had actually happened. The kiss had been brief—a contact meant to comfort, she did not doubt. Yet it had been so much more than that to her. It had shattered her; brought her somehow to life—to a tremulous intense awareness of him as a man and of her own longing for close, warm contact. It had brought some of the dilemmas of her life into an even sharper focus. . .

The first person she saw in the nurses' locker room early in the morning was Angie.

'Hi, Angie! How are you?' They hugged each other. 'You look better than you did when I saw you last. How's everything?'

'Oh, I've sort of come to terms with it, you know. . .' Angie said, her wobbly voice giving the lie to her assertion. 'I've talked to people who knew him—our friends at school. Anyway, I want to look forward, not back, at this moment. Are you here for the same reason that I'm here? To see our transplant patient before we start for the day?'

'Yes. Shall we go up there together?'

'Sure. The donor's name was John Lunt,' Angie said, as she stepped deftly into her scrub suit. 'I think it will make me feel better to see that John's liver is giving someone else a new life. . . It sort of makes it right.'

'She's off the ventilator and doing well—Dr Richardson told me that yesterday—but still heavily sedated,' Elaine assured her.

From that time on, starting with the brief visit to the intensive care unit to see Linda Ostey, the day proved to be hectic, broken only by late and short breaks for coffee and a hasty lunch and ending with their being off duty three-quarters of an hour late.

'See you guys tomorrow bright and early,' Jill Parkes told her team as they were finally leaving. 'If you think today was bad take a look at Dr Kenton's list for tomorrow! What he hasn't got on there isn't worth knowing about!'

The operating list for Dr Kenton was long and complex. Cathy, Angie and Elaine crowded round it in the unit prep room. Nobody said anything; they simply looked at each other, exchanging meaningful glances.

'Goodnight, kids,' Elaine said, the first to move. 'Sleep tight. You're going to need it.' As she hurried to the locker room, eager to get home, she felt a twinge of a kind of excited apprehension. Would Raoul Kenton be any different towards her? Show a regret that he had broken through a professional barrier? Well, she for one was not going to be any different. . .

Dr Kenton operated several times a week, usually for a whole day. At a quarter past seven the next morning Elaine stood looking at the operating list once again for Unit 2. Every room in the operating suite was to be in use that day, as they were on most days.

Already the whole place was humming with purposeful activity as all the operating room nurses came in to work more or less at the same time, swarming down the main corridor from the locker rooms or the nurses' coffee-lounge to go to their respective units where they would be working for the day. Elaine ran a practised eye once again down the list that was for Raoul Kenton in her unit, plus the list for Dr Pearce Samuels who was booked in the adjoining room.

'Glad you're not going to scrub for old Sammy today, eh?' Cathy Stravinsky had come to join her. She grinned at Elaine before tying on her face mask. 'Angie's got him today. So it's just you and me with the great Dr Kenton. Aren't we the lucky ones?'

'I'm with you there, Cathy!' Elaine grinned, wondering whether the astute Cathy would pick up any vibes from her about how her feelings for Raoul Kenton were changing.

'The last time I scrubbed for old Sammy,' Cathy said, 'I was so nervous waiting for him to start ranting and raving I kept dropping stuff all over the place. He waited about ten seconds before he started shouting.' Cathy had a thin, intelligent face, with expressive dark eyes. Her wry sense of humour was perfect for the working life of the operating room.

'Hmm,' Elaine grinned back. 'At least Jill knows how to deal with him and she gets better at it all the time. I heard her say to him the other day, "Relax, Dr Samuels, we're not doing a brain transplant here, you know!"'

'That's great,' Cathy laughed. 'I'll have to make some reference to that some time. Even he must have a sense of humour, buried deep.'

'Maybe one day soon the Dr Samuels of this world will be a dying breed,' Elaine commented.

'I'm not holding my breath waiting.' Cathy came to look at the list over her shoulder. 'Shall we take turns scrubbing? Have you any preferences?'

'I'd like to scrub for that exploratory laparotomy, if you don't mind, Cathy,' she said. 'It should be interesting.'

'Sure,' Cathy agreed readily.

'OK, then,' Elaine said cheerfully, 'let's put ourselves in purdah and get a move on. A good thing we love our jobs, isn't it?'

Between the two of them they prepared the room

for the first operation. The evening and night staff had stocked the room with all the equipment they would need; all they had to do was open up. They would begin operating at eight o'clock sharp, which meant that the patient had to be in the room ready for the anaesthetic about ten minutes before that at least. Elaine would be scrubbed and well on the way to having her sterile set-up ready.

She was doing just that when Dr Kenton opened the door and looked in. 'Hi, Cathy. . . Hi, Elaine,' he said. 'Making good progress, I see.'

'We sure are,' Cathy spoke up, 'so don't you guys keep us waiting.'

'I wouldn't think of it,' he said. 'I'll be ready when you are.'

Elaine paused in her tasks to peer at him myopically through her goggles, which tended to obscure distance vision. He smiled at her slightly, then turned to leave the room as their patient was wheeled in for the exploratory laparotomy.

Matt Ferrera was the first surgeon to come in from the scrub sinks. 'How are you, *cara mia*?' he said to her as she handed him a sterile towel, his dark eyes warm with their usual flirtatious humour.

'I'm fine, Matt,' she said, holding a sterile gown open for him to put his arms into. 'The same as usual. I guess things will be hectic for us until about a week before Christmas. . .all those surgeons wanting to do as many cases as possible before the holiday.'

'Talking of Christmas,' he said, thrusting a hand firmly into the latex glove that she now held open for him, 'the Christmas party will be coming up soon. Want to come with me again, *cara*?' As he spoke Raoul Kenton came into the room.

'Mmm, why not?' Elaine murmured hastily, knowing that Dr Kenton had heard the remark. Several times she had gone to hospital parties with Matt. They both liked each other a lot, although they also knew that there was nothing serious between them. Matt was far too busy concentrating on his career to have much time for romance, while she had been content with that. An essential spark was missing from their relationship— the spark of passion and the possibility of a deep love.

When Matt moved away from her Dr Kenton took his place. As she handed him a towel she felt his eyes on her and she avoided meeting his glance. For some reason she didn't want him to think that she was having an affair with Matt Ferrera.

'Nice to see you scrubbed for me again, Miss Stewart. And how are you?' he asked softly. As though he really cared, she thought. She had developed a certain protective cynicism over the years in dealing with her medical colleagues, especially with the charms of attractive males.

'I'm fine now, thanks,' she said, concentrating on her duties more diligently than necessary. 'Mrs Ostey seems to be doing well.'

'She *is* doing well. There's every indication that the liver is working as it should. No signs of rejection yet,' he answered her. 'We may be doing a series of needle biopsies of the liver for the pathologist to look at to make quite sure everything's OK. So far the liver-function tests are great so the biopsies might not be necessary. I'll keep you informed,' he said crisply.

Lunch was very late for Elaine because the exploratory laparotomy took a long time and she had elected to have lunch after it was finished as she had really wanted to scrub for the case.

'Can I have a word, Elaine, before you go for lunch?' Jill Parkes waylaid her outside Unit 2 just as she was removing her mask prior to leaving her unit to go to the nurses' lounge to have the packed lunch that she had brought from home. 'Come into the clean prep room for a moment.'

Wondering what it was all about, Elaine followed Jill through a door into the prep room for their unit. No one else was there. The room housed a small autoclave for sterilising instruments—by very hot steam under pressure—between cases. They also kept sterile packs there for the next cases.

'What is it?' Elaine asked curiously. Jill was seldom mysterious like this.

'Dr Kenton has asked me to tell you that he thinks you ought to be off the liver transplant team for at least a month,' Jill said in a rush, her face flushing slightly. 'I'm sorry I have to be the one to tell you. . .I didn't want to.'

'Oh, God,' Elaine groaned, her heart giving a sudden leap of shock. 'Did he say exactly why?' She was beginning to guess but wanted to hear it in exact words.

'He said you fainted the other night; that he thinks you're absolutely exhausted and need a break,' Jill said.

'Yes, I did faint.' Elaine's eyes opened wide with amazement. 'It was just due to lack of food. . .I was hypoglycaemic. . .that's all. Yes, I was tired. Aren't we all?'

'It doesn't mean that you'll be off the team permanently—maybe just until the new year,' Jill said, with an air of apology tinged with mild reproach. 'You should have told me, Elaine. You could have taken a few more days off. I could have got someone to stand in for you.'

'Thanks, Jill,' she said, a gamut of emotions confusing her. 'He. . . Dr Kenton. . .was so kind to me when I fainted. He drove me home. I didn't expect him to react like this now. . .wanting me off the team.' She did not think that she could tell Jill that he had also cooked a meal for her; had kissed her. 'A lot of nurses would

like to be on that team and if I go I may not be able to
get back on again. Do you think it would do any good
if I spoke to him? Tried to reason with him? It's not as
though I'm going to be incompetent.'

'I don't think it would do much good but you can
try,' Jill said, with sympathy. 'He said he would make
sure that you stayed on the team. He said that we needn't
mention it to the nursing co-ordinator yet; we'll just
keep it to ourselves because he doesn't think we'll get
another transplant case before Christmas anyway.
Maybe you do need a break, Elaine. Maybe it's a
good idea.'

'No. . .I think it would be better for me if I carried on.
I must speak to him. . .' She felt some of her equilibrium
deserting her.

'It's because he's understanding that he's suggesting
this. I think you should look at it in that light,' Jill said.
'He also suggested that Angie should be off the team
until the new year—when he found out that she knew
the donor.'

'Does Angie know that?'

'Yes, I've told her. She seems relieved, actually,' Jill
said. 'Go have your lunch now. If you want to talk about
it to him you could go up to see him in his private office
on the fourth floor after work if you can get past the
secretary up there—you know what she's like! Anyway,
I must get back to work now. I'll see you later. Don't
worry too much and let me know how it turns out. It
has nothing to do with your competence.'

Elaine waited in the prep room for a few moments
after Jill had gone, trying to compose her features which
felt tight with shock. There was a sense that Raoul
Kenton had let her down; had betrayed her, even though
Jill could be right that he was simply being understanding. From his point of view she supposed that he could
be concerned that she did not have the stamina to keep

going. Well, he was wrong. And she would have to tell him so at the earliest opportunity. Over a quick lunch she would decide how to deal with the situation—and Raoul Kenton.

During the remainder of the working day she avoided direct eye contact with Dr Kenton. Whenever she inadvertently met his glance she looked away again quickly, sure that he must see anguish and accusation in her regard.

When she was finally off duty she put on her lab coat and went immediately to the fourth floor, assuming that he would have gone to his offices. It was there that he saw a few out-patients in the late afternoon. Several doctors shared the same area; they also shared a secretary, a 'dragon lady' who guarded her doctors jealously.

Elaine waited until the secretary had to answer the telephone, then walked briskly through the waiting-room and down a corridor to a door that was marked with the name of the man she was looking for. Fully expecting the secretary to come running after her, she immediately knocked firmly on the door.

'Come in.'

Without giving herself time to think or to rehearse again what she had planned to say she opened the door and went in. The thudding of her heart reminded her of how scared she really felt.

To him she would probably be just another nurse— a small cog in the big machine of the vast surgical unit and someone who could be replaced. Right now she began to doubt that he would even notice if she were to disappear off the face of the earth, in spite of the fact that he had obviously wanted to kiss her. . .had done so. However, to her the job was precious—particularly her job on the transplant team—and she intended to fight for it if necessary to make herself noticed.

He was seated at a wide desk, his back to a window

and the waning daylight highlighting his extraordinary pale hair. As Elaine covered the small space between the door and the desk her mind momentarily went blank. As she strove to find opening words he certainly did not avoid looking at her; his tawny, enigmatic eyes seemed to bore right into her as he waited for her to speak.

Moments ticked by. When she did not break the silence he did it for her. 'I was rather expecting you. . . Elaine,' he said. Then she felt dwarfed as he rose to his feet and came round the desk to stand near her. Involuntarily she took a step back. The expression on his face was unreadable, to say the least.

'I don't want to be off the liver transplant team,' she said, more abruptly and challengingly than she had originally intended. 'I understand that you want me off it.'

'I don't want you off it; definitely not,' he said, narrowing his eyes at her as though to assess her mood before proceeding, 'You're a great scrub nurse. I simply think it would be better for you to take a break because it seems to me you're exhausted. I've had that on my mind ever since you fainted. I'm not considering so much my own team—I'm also considering Pearce Samuels. You and I would be fine. Samuels can be a real boor, to put it politely. I'm sure I don't have to go into that with you, do I?'

'No,' she said quietly, thrown off course by this unexpected tack. On the days that she did not work with Raoul Kenton she sometimes worked with Pearce Samuels, a middle-aged, irascible man of the old school who seemed to think that nurses were there to be handmaidens to him and, more upsetting, to be there as scapegoats when he was under stress and felt like shouting at someone.

'Guys like him are very gradually being put in their

places by the human rights department here,' Raoul Kenton remarked. 'It's going to take time.'

'It's mainly that I don't want to lose my position on the team,' she explained, forcing herself to meet his probing regard. 'There's quite a lot of competition to get on it in the first place. If the nursing co-ordinator is told that you want me to take a break she might take me out of that service completely. . .and I couldn't go back to the renal team because I was just filling in for someone else there who was off on maternity leave. She came back two months ago. . .'

'Hmm. . .' he said broodingly, 'It's certainly not my intention to take you off the team permanently. Look. . . we have no patients admitted at the moment who are status six, either for me or Dr Samuels. It's very unlikely that we'll have a candidate for a transplant before Christmas. . .although there is Carla Ritter, who's not well. I may be forced to admit her; to do something about her sooner than I'd hoped. You know Mrs Ritter, I assume?'

'Yes,' she said, moistening her dry lips with her tongue, 'I think the whole hospital knows Mrs Ritter.'

'Yes, you're probably right. As you know, she has primary biliary cirrhosis. Basically she's a very sick woman who has, in the past, refused a transplant. Very soon she may have no other choice. But right now, Elaine, I'm concerned about you.'

There was a gentle concern in his tone that made her, to her horror, lower her eyes from his face to somewhere around the middle of his broad chest to hide the sudden emotional vulnerability that came over her. 'I appreciate your concern,' she said quickly. 'Put that way, I don't really have an alternative but to go along with what you've suggested. I would like to have some sort of assurance that I can remain on the team.'

'Perhaps we could just leave it that if there's a case

that comes up for me, you'll do it; if there's a case for Pearce Samuels, you won't do it. How about that?' Unexpectedly he reached forward and lifted her face up, with one finger under her chin, so that she had to look at him—so that he could see the vulnerability and relief in her eyes. Quickly she jerked her head back— away from his touch.

'You're a great OR nurse; no dispute there,' he said, smiling crookedly at her and raising his eyebrows a little at her sudden withdrawal. 'The nursing co-ordinator has not been told about your need of a break. Only Jill Parkes knows and, as far as I'm concerned, we can leave it that way.'

'All right.' Elaine managed to get the words out, feeling an overwhelming sense of relief. 'Thank you.'

'Would you like to come with me now to the intensive care unit to see Linda Ostey?' He looked at his wrist-watch with a quick, decisive flick of his arm. 'I've seen my last patient here.'

'Yes, I would like to see her again,' she agreed, 'even though I did visit her this morning. And I would sure like to exit with you so that I don't have a run-in with the dragon lady.'

'The. . .who?'

'The—um—secretary out there. I call her the ''dragon lady'',' she explained rather sheepishly. 'One can never get past her without some sort of argument.'

'Hmm. . .' Dr Kenton looked amused '. . .I don't exactly see Ms Marchant in that light but I do take your point. She's not that way with me.'

'Well, she wouldn't be, would she?' Elaine said hotly, thinking of the imperious way that Ms Marchant and those of her ilk dealt with the most simple, the most polite, request from a young nurse, particularly if that nurse happened to be pretty.

Then she realised the implications of her words and

began to blush, the sudden heat fuelled by the way that Raoul Kenton was looking at her, amusement in his dark eyes and a slight smile on his sensual mouth.

Very clearly she could see that he understood her only too well; that the Ms Marchants of the hospital world were seldom rude or imperious with staff surgeons, particularly those as powerfully and sexually attractive as Dr Kenton. He was not conceited, just very aware of a particular type of sycophantic behaviour to which his breed were sometimes subjected—a kind of simpering worship from afar. It was an occupational hazard.

Thinking about it, Elaine hoped fervently that she would never be in the position to have to find affection and vicarious mental sex from afar. No, she wanted the real thing.

Momentarily, looking at him, she allowed herself to wonder what it would be like to be crushed in the arms of Raoul Kenton in a passionate embrace; to be pulled against the firmness of his chest; to feel loved and wanted by him in every sense of those words. . .something different from the gentle, comforting kiss he had given her the other night. She allowed herself to think of his mouth on hers, moving warmly, exploring. . .

Then she sobered up quickly. Perhaps she was already becoming somewhat like Ms Marchant; perhaps that was how it started. . .

She swallowed hard. 'Thank you,' she said, then repeated herself, 'Yes, I would like to come to see Mrs Ostey.'

The room had become too claustrophobic for the two of them and she walked to the door and fumbled with the knob to pull it open. There was an atmosphere of awareness that she found disturbing. As attractive as she found this man, she did not want to get emotionally involved with him: that way disaster lay. . .for her if not for him.

She did not think for one moment that he would consider her seriously as a romantic or sexual prospect. Not that she undervalued herself or thought that he was any sort of snob; it was just that he was a whizz kid at the hospital, as doctors were known there who became very successful at a relatively young age. She supposed him to be about thirty-five.

Men like him generally had their pick of the available women in the hospital, of whom there were many in a hospital the size of this one. Rumour had it that he was 'going out' with Dr Della Couts, a physician on the medical side of the team that dealt with liver transplants—the ones who made the initial diagnoses of liver disease and referred patients to surgeons.

Ms Marchant opened her eyes very wide as they went past her, giving Elaine a sharp, questioning look. Dr Kenton forestalled any comment by smiling at her and saying, 'Goodnight, Ms Marchant.'

'Goodnight, Doctor.'

On the way to the intensive care unit Dr Kenton talked to her about primary biliary cirrhosis, the disease from which Carla Ritter suffered. Everyone in the hospital who was connected with the liver disease clinic and the transplant team knew Carla, a middle-aged woman who was terrified of having a liver transplant and had put off the inevitable as long as possible.

'It sounds as though the disease has finally caught up with her.' Elaine offered the comment as she hurried to keep pace with him. 'That a transplant is inevitable.'

'I'm afraid so,' he said as they walked briskly along a hospital corridor. 'There is some evidence that it might be an auto-immune disease, where body chemicals in the liver actually destroy the bile ducts. So there isn't much we can do other than a transplant.'

'Yes,' she said, speaking firmly, 'I have done a fair amount of reading on it. I guess I know most of the theory.' There was no way that she wanted him to have the assumption that she did her job blind, so to speak, and that she didn't know all the reasons why a particular operation was being performed in the operating room.

'That's great,' he said.

Mrs Ostey was in a room of her own in the intensive care unit.

'You'll notice a definite improvement in her colour,' Dr Kenton said as they approached the room, putting a hand on Elaine's upper arm as though to reassure her, 'but she still looks quite ill. It's been an ordeal for her. She's as comfortable as we can make her.'

As they went through the doorway of the room they saw that Dr Della Couts and a nurse were with Mrs Ostey. Dr Couts was entering data into the computer that was near the bedside, information that would go directly into the patient's medical file.

'Hi there, Dell!' Raoul Kenton said in a familiar way to Dr Couts, apparently very pleased to see his medical colleague there, whose job it was to monitor their patient's blood-clotting function and other vital functions to make sure that her body chemistry was returning to normal and that the new liver was functioning. It was necessary to take frequent blood samples for this.

Dr Couts had a vivid, dark beauty. Even when she had most of her dark, wavy hair covered and a face mask on, as she did now, there was a vivacity about her that was striking. 'Hi, Raoul. How are you?' she said, smiling at him, then looking at the hand that he still had on Elaine's upper arm. Somehow her glance did not quite get to Elaine herself. Contrasted with her hair and the eyes that were almost black, her pale skin had the look and apparent texture of creamy magnolia petals.

Elaine pulled away from Dr Kenton to go up to the

near side of the high bed on which Linda Ostey lay, feeling herself to be more or less invisible as Dr Couts began to discuss medical matters with Dr Kenton; she had, after all, come to see the patient. Nevertheless, she felt herself to be somehow dismissed.

The woman looked small and vulnerable in the bed, her face drawn and haggard as she lay immobile with her eyes closed. A gastric tube protruded from one nostril, attached to a mechanical pump. Leads went from her chest to the computerised monitors beside the bed. Another tube drained urine from her bladder. Two intravenous lines dripped fluid and drugs into her veins.

While coming up there, Elaine had entertained the idea that she would be able to say a few words to Mrs Ostey this time. When she and Angie had visited earlier their patient had been asleep. It would be gratifying at least to be able to ask her how she was feeling and to get a brief reply. Now Elaine saw that it was not going to be possible. This woman was much sicker than some of her previous patients had been following kidney transplants.

'How is she?' she whispered to the nurse, while the two doctors continued their quiet, intense conversation on the other side of the bed.

'She's OK,' the other nurse said after a considered hesitation. 'This is about what you would expect. She's holding her own. The liver seems to be doing all right.'

Quite suddenly, as she stared down at their patient still battling for her life and still not out of the woods, so to speak, Elaine had a vision of Angie Clark's stricken face as she had confided to Elaine that she knew the donor. Out of the tragedy of a young man's death this woman, fighting courageously to stay alive, had another chance. Somehow, it seemed to Elaine then that Linda Ostey was fighting for the young man's life as well, in a way: if she succeeded, part of him would go on living. An unexplainable emotion filled her.

After a few more minutes Elaine left the room quietly and headed back towards the elevators. The liver was such a vital organ in the body—it performed so many important functions that were necessary to survival as well as to good health—that these crucial days were witnessing a life or death struggle.

'Elaine. . .wait!' Dr Kenton had come out of the room and was walking rapidly towards her as she waited for the elevator.

Impulsively, affecting not to have heard him, she decided not to wait for an elevator. Pulling open a door to the stairwell, she went through quickly and began to run down the long flights of stairs. Not normally an envious person, the sight of Raoul Kenton being so familiar with Dr Della Couts had elicited a sharp stab of envy in her of which she was ashamed. The emotion frightened her, too.

Silently she admonished him as she ran from him: You shouldn't have kissed me. . . You shouldn't have touched me!

It was too late: the damage was done. . .

That evening Angie telephoned. 'Can we meet soon, Elaine? I'd like to talk to someone. I hear from Jill that you may be off the team, like me.'

'Yes. Come over here Friday evening,' Elaine offered. 'Come for supper. I'll cook something good. . . get a bottle of wine. We could rent a video—maybe a comedy. I could use a good laugh.'

'You're on,' Angie agreed. 'I'll get the video.'

'This is great—just what I needed,' Angie commented on the Friday evening as she sat with her elbows on the dining-table that Elaine had in one corner of the sitting-room at her flat. Angie was on her third glass of

Chianti. 'You're an absolute whizz in the kitchen, Elaine. Has anyone ever told you that?' Angie's unruly ginger hair was held back from her face in a ponytail, and she wore a casual sweatshirt and jeans.

'A few, from time to time.' Similarly attired, Elaine lounged back in the chair opposite, mellowed with wine and thinking of that previous meal she had shared with Dr Kenton.

'I needed to get a few things off my chest,' Angie said. 'Thanks for always being there when I need someone; thanks for listening.'

'That's what friends are for. Isn't that what we always say?'

They both began to giggle, as though at some sort of 'in' joke. At work they protected each other as best they could from the onslaughts of bad-tempered surgeons; when such an attack was successfully subverted they would quip, 'Isn't that what friends are for?'

'Even so, Elaine. . .' Angie sobered up for a moment, '. . .I'm sorry to dump all that on you.'

'Don't mention it. You'll be doing the same for me one day, don't you worry!' Elaine's face was flushed from the wine, her large grey eyes alight with laughter. 'It's great to have a natter about all the guys at work. . . to let it all hang out.' As though on cue they both began to giggle again. 'I don't think we're going to need that comic video after all.'

'What's with you and Matt?' Angie asked, getting the words out between gasps for air. 'Are you going to marry the guy?'

'No,' Elaine said emphatically. 'For one thing he hasn't asked me. . .'

'That's a point,' Angie said.

Elaine grinned back at her. 'Will you shut up a minute?' she said. 'Sometimes I wonder what it would be like to be married to Matt. He's one of eight offspring. . .' She thought of Matt's noisy, affectionate, ebullient family. 'Sometimes I feel I would love to be part of that family, Angie, since I'm one of only two myself. Then at other times I realise that I would probably get lost in the crowd. I think Matt would definitely put his family before me. . .'

She gazed musingly into space, toying with her wine glass, her thoughts sliding back to Raoul Kenton. 'I don't want to take second place with the man I marry. Besides, I don't love Matt.'

What would marriage to Raoul Kenton be like? The thought came to her without conscious volition. He certainly had an intensity, an enigmatic quality, that Matt did not have. Would a wife take second place to his work? Obviously his first wife had not found him perfect.

'Is there anything between you and Raoul Kenton?' Angie said astutely, in spite of being partially inebriated. 'I think I've picked up vibes. He watches you a lot, and I don't think it's anything to do with the job.'

There was no point in lying to her friend, Elaine knew, especially as her face was becoming even more flushed than it had been before. Angie was trustworthy and did not betray a confidence.

'Well, if you must know. . . When he brought me home that night he. . .he kissed me.'

'Yikes!'

'I don't think it meant anything,' she said hastily, 'at least not to him.'

'I'm not so sure,' Angie said. 'I don't suppose he distributes his affections lightly.' She leaned forward across the table. 'I said I would fill you in about his past, didn't I? Well. . .his wife left him after their child died, so I heard. She must have been crazy.'

'It's a common phenomenon, so I believe,' Elaine said. 'They remind each other too much of the pain. . .

afterwards. And they can't comfort each other much because they're both suffering. If it happened to me. . .I don't know what I'd do.'

'Have some more wine. . .' Angie picked up the bottle of Chianti and filled Elaine's glass '. . .otherwise we're going to need that video pronto. Anyway, he's a fantastic guy. Maybe he's in your cards.'

'No.'

'You've got a lot to offer a man. . .personality, intelligence, charm. . .you're attractive. . .still waters run deep and all that.'

'Oh, go on. . .'

'It's true,' Angie insisted. 'You have a certain genuine warmth, tempered with a rather rare common sense.'

'I don't think I'd know what to do, Angie. . .with him,' she said.

'Don't do anything,' Angie said. 'Let it come to you. If he wants to, he'll come.'

'I wonder if he's still in contact with his wife. . . whether they divorced?' Elaine mused, aware of niggles of feelings something like jealousy and not liking herself for them.

'Oh, I'm pretty sure they divorced. Shall I ask him when next we meet?' Angie offered facetiously, giggling again.

'You know, Angie,' Elaine said thoughtfully, changing the subject as though she had a premonition that the next liver transplant would somehow bring her closer to Raoul Kenton—or the opposite, 'that Carla Ritter's been admitted to the hospital? It's now or never for her, apparently. She'll be a status six patient, for sure. So it looks like we'll get another transplant before Christmas. . .provided we get a donor.'

'Yes, I knew she was in,' Angie said, more soberly. 'Poor Carla. She's such a skinny little woman but such a fighter, too. I feel for her, I really do. She's got a ten-year-old daughter, you know, as well as older kids. That's why she didn't want to have a transplant. She wanted to go on as long as possible without it; she thought it would be less risky.'

'It sure isn't less risky now,' Elaine said. 'She doesn't have a choice any more.'

'Well, it will be your show, kid. I guess Raoul will let you scrub with him. I'm definitely off the team until the new year.'

'You know, Angie, I feel as though my life has changed somehow since I was involved with that first transplant,' she said, looking at her friend intently, her elbows on the table. 'Maybe it had something to do with your knowing the donor. I feel I'm not so self-centred, somehow.'

'Yeah, I know what you mean.'

'Before that I was so preoccupied with how hard I was working; with how all-consuming the job had become. I was so anxious about the implications of that for the future. You know, cutting yourself off from the possibility of husband and children.'

'Yeah, tell me about it!' Angie said, rolling her eyes upward. 'It's called growing up; it's getting scared that you can't have everything just like you thought you could; that maybe you can't even have a career *and* marriage and children. What can you do? You just have to go with the flow. If you get offered promotion, or want promotion, you just have to "play it by ear".'

'Mmm. The inevitable ticking of the biological clock,' Elaine murmured, 'that gets louder with each passing year.' It was a familiar and common concern, she knew, among women—of how to reconcile the inevitable ticking of that clock with the greater and greater demands of an absorbing career. 'Some women make a more or less conscious choice one way or the other. . .'

'Yeah. And some just let themselves drift with time,' Angie chipped in, 'avoiding the issue until something brings them up short. What sort are you, kid?'

'Oh. . .I guess I'm just a drifter,' Elaine said, trying to make light of it, 'waiting for the right man before I confront the issue.'

Cornelius interrupted their dialogue by jumping up onto Elaine's lap, purring loudly, and she gathered him up into her arms. 'Hullo, Cornelius, my love,' she crooned, nuzzling his soft fur. 'He's reminding us that there are other things beside work, Angie.'

'Right!' Angie said, jumping up. 'I'll put on that video.'

CHAPTER FOUR

THE call came two weeks later, just four weeks before Christmas. Elaine was on her way home from work when her pager went off.

As she expected it was the number of the organ transplant service co-ordinator, Bill Radnor, that was displayed on the pager when she checked—the service known at the hospital as the MOR, short for Multiple Organ Retrieval Service. It was barely four o'clock in the afternoon.

First she had to establish the time of the proposed operation—to find out whether she had time to continue on home, to have a bath and to cook herself supper. Getting herself to a public telephone as quickly as she could, she punched in the familiar number.

He answered after only one ring. 'MOR office,' he said tersely, 'Bill Radnor.'

She always experienced a certain sense of awe when she spoke to Bill, who spent his days, and often his nights, in a small, cluttered office at University Hospital, surrounded by computers. From there he co-ordinated the entire organ transplant service for the hospital and, together with a handful of operatives in other teaching centres, for the whole province. It was Bill who matched up donors and recipients for their hospital over this wide-ranging area. It was Bill who started the main ball rolling.

'Hello, Bill,' she said. 'It's Elaine Stewart, the OR nurse, answering my page.'

'Hello, Elaine.' His voice warmed instantly. 'All

systems go for tonight. Eight-thirty. Tentative time at the moment. Dr Kenton's case.'

'OK, Bill,' she said, feeling the familiar respect.

'Jill Parkes wants you to call her, Elaine, as usual,' Bill was saying, 'Then she'll confirm the final time with you later. What's all this about you being off the liver team, except for Dr Kenton, until the new year?'

'Oh. . .he thinks I'm too tired to carry on or something.'

'Ha! If we're going on tired, that would wipe out the whole team!' There was an ironical note in his chuckle.

'Is it Carla Ritter, Bill?' she asked.

'Yep, it's Carla. At last,' he said, the sadness of inevitability in his voice. 'She can't put it off any longer.'

'No. . .' Elaine agreed feelingly. 'Poor Carla! I feel as though we've come to the end of a countdown, Bill. I bet she does, too.'

'You bet!' he said. 'Maybe she thought she could hold the disease off by sheer will-power. No will-power could halt the march of *that* disease. Anyway. . .where are you, Elaine? Sounds like you're on a subway station.'

'I am. Just on my way home.'

Just as well Bill wasn't married, she thought. It wouldn't be much of a life for a partner. Not for the first time Elaine wondered how long it would take him to burn out. He was young for such responsibility— only twenty-seven.

'I can think of worse places to be than on the subway,' Bill laughed, 'and, believe me, I've heard them all!'

'I bet you have! Thanks, Bill. Bye.'

Jill took longer to answer the telephone than Bill had done. When she did she was breathless.

'Hello, it's me. . . Elaine.'

'Hi, Elaine,' Jill said calmly. 'Bill rounded you up pretty quick! Sorry you had to leave the hospital before

I got to you. "Go" time is probably around eight-thirty, as I guess Bill would have said. I'll call you to confirm as soon as I'm sure. You going to be at home?'

'Yes. And I'll be driving back when I come.'

'Great! You're going to be on Raoul Kenton's team, the recipient team. I believe the donor liver's coming from someplace else. . .flying in. They're doing Mrs Ritter, the one in Critical Care. You know her, I guess? She's in no great shape.'

'Yes, I know her,' Elaine said. 'In fact, I went to see her today.'

'Call you later, then. Bye.'

The memory of the visit to Mrs Ritter came sharply to Elaine's mind as she continued her journey home. It was a good thing, she thought now, that nurses on the transplant teams were required to visit and learn about possible organ recipients who were on the waiting lists. That visit had certainly made her understand the issues all right. . .and the potential problems that could arise during operations and in the recovery period. To her, now, Carla Ritter was a person and not just a case. The woman was desperately ill; jaundiced, weak from blood-clotting problems and other problems of a disordered metabolism caused by her disease.

Hardly aware of her surroundings, Elaine got off the train and walked the familiar route to her flat. As she walked, the mid-November chill penetrated her wool coat, making her shiver. Pale yellow leaves that had fallen from the mature maple trees that grew along the street were plastered to the sidewalk by rain water. Other leaves floated gently around her from above, settling like snowflakes.

Cornelius, whom she adored, would be waiting for her and waiting for his dinner. She acknowledged wryly that the cat was a substitute child for her. . .or a substitute something. She wanted someone to love; someone to love her in return. Instead, her life was filled with work, all-absorbing work, that left little time for anything else. Sometimes she felt that her work was consuming her, devouring her. It was no less consuming because she loved it, basically. Perhaps loving it made her more vulnerable—always available; never calling in sick.

An image of Raoul Kenton, whom she would be seeing again in a few hours, came to her then, bringing with it, strangely, an unfamiliar, nostalgic ache in the region of her heart. Oh, God. . .don't let me make a fool of myself with him! Yet the prospect of being with him soon brought a kind of peace and an all-consuming excitement.

The largest part of her mind was still on the forthcoming operation. Not a good operation risk. . .that was Mrs Ritter. And they would all be very, very aware of it.

The telephone call came from Jill Parkes while Elaine was eating her supper. 'We're scheduled to go at eight-thirty, definite,' Jill said. 'We'll be in our own rooms. You'll be scrubbing on your own, Elaine. . . The other girl I wanted to get has gone down with flu. . .the same as about one third of the entire OR staff, from what I hear. Sorry about that but there's nothing I can do. Just give yourself a good hour to get ready—that's the best thing.'

'All right.'

'The donor liver's coming in from Montreal by private jet so we might have a bit of leeway there timewise. Cathy and I will be circulating. OK?' Jill said, speaking at breakneck speed.

'Sure. I'll be there in the room by seven-fifteen, sharp. Unless you want me there earlier?' Elaine answered.

'No, that's fine. And don't worry, kid. We'll be right there with you.' Jill hung up.

They had a refined, organised routine in the operating

rooms, which each member of the teams knew inside out and backwards, both medical teams and both nursing teams. From now on Elaine was on a kind of countdown, watching the clock. Her time was definitely not her own. There was an inevitability about the coming events now. She herself was a cog in the machinery.

Their patient, not far from death, would be waiting to receive the gift of another chance at life. One person would die, was already brain-dead; one would live. Long before now both the recipient and the donor would have been tissue-typed, determined by a blood test, to make sure that they were a good match. Both of them would have been given doses of the immuno-suppressive drug, Cyclosporine, which would help to prevent the body of the recipient patient from rejecting the donor liver. Elaine knew that her part of the operation would take about eight hours.

Cathy Stravinsky was already in the OR locker room when Elaine got there later, pulling on one of the light blue, one-piece scrub suits.

'Hi, Elaine,' Cathy greeted her, smiling in her quiet, welcoming way. ' "Once more unto the breach," and all that!'

'You said it, Cath!' Elaine grinned, helping herself to a scrub suit from a pile, then opening her locker.

'You know they're doing Carla? I don't give much for her chances.'

'I'll be praying every bit of the way, I can tell you, Cath. Thank God it's Raoul Kenton.'

'Yeah, you can say that again!' Cathy said with feeling, as she slipped her feet hurriedly into her white operating shoes. 'I'll go in there and make a start opening up the packs, Elaine. Jill will be up to her eyeballs. See you in there.' Like a whirlwind she was gone, letting the door slam behind her.

As Elaine pushed every stray wisp of hair up into an unflattering cap in front of the mirror, she thought of their patient. They seldom had to operate on someone as debilitated as Carla. Somewhere in the hospital Carla's family would be gathering; a ten-year-old girl would be saying goodbye to her mother, a goodbye that could be the last she would ever say to the woman she loved above all others. Each member of the staff and the transplant team would be constantly mindful of those waiting people. . .waiting. . .waiting. . .with a dreadful fear in their hearts vying with the hope.

Taking a deep, steadying breath, Elaine left the locker room. It had taken her less than four minutes to change. Quickly she walked the short distance to the double doors of the main operating suite. She would be up all night, powered by adrenalin and the addictive excitement that operating-room nurses felt when they knew they were in the front line of action.

With the other individuals who made up her team— Raoul Kenton, Mike Richardson, Matt Ferrera, Tony Asher, Claude Moreau et al., Jill and Cathy—she would be doing her best, her very best, to ensure that if it was humanly possible to save Carla Ritter they would save her.

CHAPTER FIVE

'She's bleeding like crazy.' Mike Richardson muttered the words, articulating what they could all see, as he and Dr Kenton bent over the inert, draped form of their patient where only the operating site was exposed. Raoul Kenton had his gloved hands deep inside the abdominal cavity. For some time now the bleeding had been increasing from a steady ooze to a more alarming rate that was becoming difficult to control.

Elaine exchanged glances with Cathy, raising her eyebrows expressively while quickly pouring warm saline from a jug into a bowl of gauze sponges that she had ready. This was what they had been frightened of. . . This was what they had been waiting for with a tense expectation.

'Large sponges. . .moist. . .lots of them,' Dr Kenton said calmly, quickly, as a new atmosphere of a need for readiness made itself felt in the room like something palpable.

'Clamps, please,' Dr Richardson requested. Reaching up, he gripped the sterile handles of the two powerful operating-room lights that were positioned directly over the operating table and changed the angle of them so that he could see more clearly inside the abdominal cavity where the diseased liver was exposed. Then he took the proffered instruments to clamp off some of the oozing blood vessels.

Elaine was ready with the warm, moist sponges. . . had been for some time, just as she was ready with everything else that might be needed at a second or two's notice. The tension kept her alert and mentally agile, thinking ahead to all possibilities. In a quick flurry of activity she prepared to meet the emergency.

'How's she doing, Claude?' Dr Kenton said tersely to the anaesthetist.

'She's OK. I'll have the worst bleeding under control in a moment or two. I don't want to bring her blood pressure down any more than it is now,' Dr Moreau said, adjusting the control valves on the various intravenous lines while his assistant injected drugs.

'Jill. . .call the blood bank, please,' he went on. 'Ask them if they've cross-matched the extra four units of blood. . .and we'd better have more on standby. Get them to prepare more of the fresh-frozen plasma. In the meantime I'll have the other three units of blood you've got on hand.'

Claude and the senior anaesthesia resident stood at the head of the operating table with their complex anaesthetic machine and various electronic monitors that told them all the precise details of their patient's condition.

'Matt. . .pack a few damp sponges down in there. . . right underneath the liver. . .that's it,' Raoul Kenton instructed his assistant. 'Go easy with the suction, Tony. This liver's extremely fragile, by the look of it.'

'More sponges, Cath,' Elaine said quietly. Her throat felt tight from a fear that they could be getting into very serious trouble.

Quickly Cathy opened several packs of large, sterile sponges and placed them on Elaine's instrument table, while in the background the calm tones of Jill Parkes instructed the blood bank over the telephone. The atmosphere changed subtly in the operating room as they all shifted into a kind of mental overdrive.

'One-two-three-four-five . . . one-two-three-four-five. . .one-two-three-four-five.' Quietly, quickly, Elaine counted the bundles of sponges that Cathy had given her, while Cathy watched to confirm the number and then wrote it down on the procedure sheet. 'I'll have some more of the warm saline, Cath.'

'More sponges, please,' Dr Kenton instructed her, 'then give me two of the long, curved clamps. . .the ones with the fine tips.'

As she moved to comply Mike Richardson removed some of the used sponges that had absorbed the blood that had poured from Mrs Ritter's diseased liver as they had been carefully dissecting it out and Elaine quickly passed up a stainless-steel bowl to receive them before passing up the clamps.

'Thanks, Elaine.' Dr Kenton took the clamps, one by one, that she placed into his waiting palm. 'Then give me one of the mersilene sutures on a fine, curved needle. . .I want to do a little bit of sewing here. Keep that area dry, Matt. . .then give me a buzz with the cautery. Careful with that retractor, Tony.'

'Right,' Matt Ferrera said, his voice betraying something of the urgency to control the bleeding as he leaned over the incision in the abdominal cavity. He held a small sponge on a long sponge-holder to swab specific spots deep in the cavity.

'Here's the suture, Dr Kenton.' Elaine passed the suture on a long needle-holder, taking a quick look inside the abdominal cavity as she did so. They were a long way from getting the diseased liver out. Like everyone else in the room, no doubt, she was praying that their combined expertise would see their patient through.

'Thanks.'

'Jill. . .get on to Chemistry about those blood gases. . . They should just about be ready.' Dr Moreau was shooting off a new list of instructions. 'From the stat lab. . . OK?'

'Yeah. . .'

'Scissors. . .then more clamps. . .have some of the

fine silk ligatures ready.' Raoul Kenton's voice vied with the steady, muted whoosh and sigh of the mechanical respirator. Somehow the sound was soothing, reassuring; it kept their patient alive.

Calmly Elaine passed the lengths of silk ligatures that would be used to tie off bleeding blood vessels. She forgot herself, her own life, her worries and concerns. She forgot how much her feet and legs ached and how much she longed for a cup of coffee. Her concentration on the job was total; with the others bending over the abdominal cavity she felt herself merge into a collective psyche of intense concentration. . .like a single mind. From then on she was pure function.

The minutes ticked by tensely as each member of the team did his or her part. There was no unnecessary conversation, no unnecessary action. Each person did what they had to do, then held themselves in readiness for anything extra. With a sense of dismay Elaine watched the used sponges mount up relentlessly and glanced over at Cathy from time to time as Cathy weighed them for blood loss before spreading them out on sheets on the floor so that they could be seen clearly by both herself and the circulating nurses when they had to be counted later on.

Her eyes followed Cathy anxiously as the nurse wrote the amount of blood loss, in millilitres, on a board. Blood was pouring out faster than it was dripping into the patient's body via the intravenous lines. Then she had a vision of a little girl, Carla's daughter, waiting in the hospital for news of her mother—as well as Carla's husband and her other children.

Methodically she wrung out sponges in warm saline and passed them up to the surgeons; she mounted more sutures onto needle-holders; she lined up clamps that she knew would be needed. She felt beads of perspiration forming on her upper lip under the confining face mask, as well as along her hairline under the paper cap.

Controlling the bleeding was not easy yet control it they did, with both the anaesthetist doing things with drugs and intravenous fluids and the surgeons working at their end. As the outward flow of blood lessened there was a subtle corresponding reduction of tension in the room. Suddenly Elaine found herself giving Cathy and Jill the thumbs-up sign.

'There you had a perfect example of what primary biliary cirrhosis does to people,' Raoul Kenton explained for Tony Asher's and Elaine's benefit when the worst of the bleeding was over. For the first time in ages he took his eyes off the operation site to look at members of his team and to look at the total written blood loss on the board. 'They bleed. . .and that's because the body's blood-clotting mechanism is out of whack. The liver's a great organ. . . It does a lot for us. And we can't live without it. It also has great recuperative powers.'

'I hope we've got great recuperative powers,' Mike Richardson smiled. 'We're going to need it after this. So is Carla.'

'Get on with it, you guys,' Claude Moreau quipped. 'I don't want to be here all day as well as all night.'

'Yeah, yeah,' Dr Richardson answered back in the same tone. 'You just concentrate on passing gas, Claude. It's what you're good at.'

'Psst!' Cathy whispered to Elaine, 'I'm going to scrub to relieve you for a quick coffee-break. Make sure it's quick. I don't fancy taking this over for too long!'

'You must be psychic or something,' Elaine whispered back.

'Looks like it's doing great!' There was a note of jubilance in the voice of the otherwise sanguine Dr Claude Moreau a long time later. 'The jaundice is considerably less already. Well, guys, I guess we've made it. . .so far. I guess Carla's going to wake up to smile at us again.'

The new liver was in. It could be seen to be working before their eyes as the yellow-tinged skin of their patient was gradually changing. The healthy liver was doing its job of cleansing Carla Ritter's blood of the build-up of bile that had caused the abnormal colour.

There seemed to be a mental collective sigh as members of the surgical and anaesthesia teams looked at each other and smiled.

'Well, that was a tricky one.' Dr Kenton expressed the common feeling with superb understatement.

'Yep! We knew it would be,' Mike Richardson added.

'Let's do the first sponge count,' Cathy said to Elaine. It was time to prepare for closure.

Dawn was not far off when they transferred Carla Ritter to a special intensive-care bed and wheeled it, together with all the attendant intravenous tubing and bags of fluid, to the post anaesthesia room—otherwise known as the recovery room. She still had an endotracheal tube protruding from her mouth that would connect her to a mechanical ventilator for the next two days until the immediate crisis period was over.

As though reluctant to transfer the responsibility of their patient to others after the intensity of the operating room drama, the whole team accompanied Mrs Ritter on the short journey along the corridor. Emotions ran high. . . She had made it! So far. . .

Very soon Raoul Kenton would talk to her family; would allow them to see her briefly to assure themselves that she was indeed alive. Utterly fatigued, Elaine felt a betraying moisture gather in her eyes as she looked at the frail, vulnerable body of Carla, whose face at that moment, eyes closed beneath puffy lids, reflected years of suffering, years of anxiety. Now, perhaps, that anxiety would be over.

'Thank you for your help, Elaine.' Dr Kenton's hand was suddenly on her shoulder as she stood staring at the bed from a few yards' distance after it had been positioned in the room and the new team of nurses had gone to work connecting up the monitors to Carla Ritter. 'You were great, as always. I couldn't have wished for a better scrub nurse. I hope you found it interesting.' There was a dark growth of beard on his face that was otherwise pale and haggard. A surgical mask dangled around his neck.

'It was very interesting,' she confirmed, smiling, feeling vindicated by his praise. A facetiousness made her add: 'I was only doing my job, you know. Will Carla make it?'

'Her chances are pretty good now, I think, if we can get her over the next couple of days, provided there's no acute rejection,' he said, ignoring her riposte. 'You can see for yourself that her colour's improved considerably...the jaundice has more or less gone... which shows us that the new liver's working. We'll have to be very careful over the next hours...the next few days...to watch out for signs that her body might be rejecting the new liver, in spite of the Cyclosporine we're giving her.'

'I...I sure hope she's OK. It takes an awful lot of courage to consent to this operation, even when you know what the alternative will be,' she said.

'Yes...' he murmured agreement.

Elaine watched the night nurses, nearing the end of their shift of duty, moving quietly and methodically about their tasks of recovering patients who had been operated on during the night. There were four other patients present in the room who had required emergency surgery. Mrs Ritter would have a nurse assigned exclusively to her and Dr Moreau would be in charge during the immediate recovery period.

'Well, excuse me, Dr Kenton,' Elaine said to him, 'we've got an awful lot of clearing up to do. Goodnight. . .or good morning. . .or whatever.' There was an air of complicity between them; a something that brought them closer, having shared in a monumental effort and accomplishment. That complicity was forming a bond between them. . .she could feel its warmth.

He smiled at her crookedly, tiredly, as she turned to leave. 'Goodnight,' he said softly.

Just then Matt Ferrera came up to her with his arms open in an exaggeratedly theatrical manner and enclosed her briefly in a quick, fierce bear-hug. Such a display of emotion was common after intense hours of co-operation; he had just done the same to Jill and Cathy. 'Well done, kid,' he said, in front of the watching Dr Kenton. 'You were great!'

'Thanks, Matt,' she said, hugging him back and laughing delightedly through her haze of fatigue. 'So were you.' His dark eyes were bloodshot, his jaw covered with a growth of hair. The night was not over for Matt. He would still have to hang around to make sure that there was no immediate post-operative bleeding. She watched him move off, back to their patient's bedside.

'You're not going to faint on me again, are you?' Raoul Kenton said unexpectedly as she was about to leave, his remark hidden in the general bustle and hub-bub in the post anaesthesia room. He was looking at her with an unreadable expression in his eyes, an expression that made her feel heated with a remembrance of the way he had kissed her in her kitchen. . .and how she had responded.

'I doubt it,' she said ruefully, smiling slightly as she

pulled off the paper cap that was making her head itch and running a hand through her short, untidy hair. His eyes followed the movement. 'Although it was rather nice being fussed over.' She found herself saying the words without any sort of premeditation. Maybe her tiredness was making her less cautious about maintaining a professional distance. That distance had been breached once, anyway. . .

'How long will it take you to clear up here?' he asked.

'Oh, at least an hour,' she said, thinking of the mess of dirty instruments, linen and other equipment that the three nurses had to clear away before setting up the operating room again ready for use.

'Come down to the cafeteria in. . .' he looked at the wall clock '. . .say. . .one hour and fifteen minutes? I'll buy you breakfast—make quite sure that you don't faint driving home.'

'That's very kind of you,' she said a little awkwardly as her heart did an odd flip, thinking of the proximity that eating with him would entail again. Such proximity could lead to emotional entanglements if professional considerations were not kept strictly in mind. And she was a little in awe of him because he was so very competent in an unassuming way that inspired admiration. 'You—er—you don't have to do that.'

'I know I don't have to. I want to,' he said firmly, his voice husky as his eyes bored into hers. 'Is that a date?'

'Yes. . . Thank you,' she murmured, finding herself reddening under the intensity of his gaze. Before Matt had hugged her Dr Kenton had seemed content to let her go; the thought was disturbing, bringing with it a reluctance to dwell on possible implications.

'Raoul,' Mike Richardson called to him, 'can you come over here for a minute?'

Without another word he was gone, absorbed into the

busy scene. Several of the nurses were looking at her sharply, noting that Dr Kenton had spent more than a few minutes talking to her. They would be even more surprised, she thought, if they knew that he had asked her to share breakfast with him. Although the hospital was not exactly a hotbed of gossip such information was invariably passed on to do the rounds of the underground pipeline, part of the chat that made the wheels of human relationships go round.

Briskly Elaine walked from the room, feeling a grow- ing sense of elation, as well as a sensation of being punch-drunk. Her head ached and she longed for the feel of the cool night air on her face—to get out of the hospital. Their patient had survived. . .and so had she!

'Get stuck in!' Jill Parkes bawled as Elaine entered the chaotic operating room once again. 'I reckon every damn thing in this room that is usable has been used. . . and everything that isn't usable is splattered with blood!'

Hiding a secret glow of expectation that was at war with the old familiar apprehension where Raoul Kenton was concerned Elaine started on the instruments, sorting them out into some sort of order before they could be sent to the dirty instrument room to be washed, repacked and sterilised for future use. She had to move fast if she was to be in the cafeteria on time.

Perhaps Raoul Kenton was testing her out again—to see if she could stand the pace on his team. Certainly he had been watching her a lot, an activity that she found disconcerting, to say the least.

It was thus with apprehension, mixed with elation, that she approached the staff cafeteria. She was dressed in her outdoor clothing and was almost fifteen minutes late. On her way down there she had repeatedly glanced at her watch, wondering if he would wait for her. . .or perhaps he would not turn up himself.

The cafeteria was almost empty at this early hour of the morning. As she walked through the swinging double doors Elaine immediately saw Raoul Kenton ahead of her, carrying a tray of food, and the sight of him gave her a moment of serious doubt. Should she be doing this? Before she could retreat he had spotted her and she had no alternative but to proceed, to endure his scrutiny as he stood waiting for her to approach.

'Hi,' he said, 'I was beginning to think you had chickened out.' Like her, he had showered and shampooed his hair; he had also put on a clean scrub suit and white lab coat. His pale hair, darkened with water, was slicked down close to his head, making him look somehow boyish. Elaine found herself staring. He had shaved, too.

As she reached for a tray, he forestalled her. 'I have all our food,' he said. 'You just get two mugs of coffee. I'll pay for it. Just join me at the table.'

'All right,' she said, turning away. 'Thank you.' This had been a mistake. She felt her throat tighten up with a new kind of tension.

As much as she wanted to be with him she wasn't sure she could cope now, tired and over-worked as she was. What on earth was she going to say to him? They could not just eat in silence. Such frantic thoughts occupied her mind as she carried two mugs of scalding hot coffee over to the table where he had established himself.

She had watched him walk ahead of her; he had a way of walking that moved his whole body—a movement of lithe, purposeful ease, always appearing relaxed. It was doubtful that he was as relaxed as he appeared.

'You've chosen everything I would have picked myself,' she said, surveying the plates of pancakes with

maple syrup, the rolls of crisp bacon, the slices of canta-
loupe melon, toast and honey.

'We have similar tastes, then,' he said, his tawny
eyes alight with amusement at her enthusiasm. 'I like a
woman who gets enthusiastic about breakfast. Sit down;
let's make a start. I want to eat at least half of this before
my buzzer goes off.'

'Are you expecting it to? Is there any problem with
Carla?' she asked as she lowered herself into the chair
opposite him.

'No, nothing's wrong.' He smiled at her, the action
drawing her attention to his mouth. . .his even white
teeth. . .the memory of a kiss. 'It's just that I never seem
to get more than twenty minutes to myself, on average,
when I'm in the hospital. . .and I had hoped to have the
pleasure of your company for at least that.'

'You flatter me, Dr Kenton,' she ventured. 'Is it all
right for me to go on home now, do you think? I don't
want to leave if there's any likelihood that I'll be needed
again for Mrs Ritter.' She busied herself putting cream
in her coffee, while acutely aware of the old, worn
sweater that she was wearing with her jeans. He seemed
to miss nothing about her.

'You can go home,' he said. 'So far, things are fine.'
Unlike her, he could not go home yet; he would stay at
the hospital for some time to make quite sure that there
was no untoward post-operative bleeding in Carla
Ritter.

Sitting so close to him in this hospital setting, she
felt oddly naked without the enveloping surgical gown
and the other protective paraphernalia of her job. Like-
wise, he appeared less protected—his hair uncovered,
his slightly rugged, very masculine features on view.

'Have you. . .um. . .have you spoken to the family?'
she asked tentatively.

'Yes. They've been up all night waiting. . .including

her ten-year-old daughter. One of the few pleasures of this job is seeing their faces when you tell them all is well. Did you know Carla had a young kid?' As he spoke he passed her a plate holding three pancakes, then the jug of maple syrup.

'Yes. . .I did,' Elaine said, warming to the subject. 'I met her once—a skinny little kid, like her mother. I felt so sad for her. It's so difficult to explain to a child when what they're feeling is such intense emotion. And. . . and you don't want to be patronising.'

'I know,' he said. 'Time and experience, particularly personal experience, do make you better at it; to understand more of what other people are going through, if you are capable of such empathy in the first place. . .'

There was something in his tone that made her look up at him sharply. The haunted, guarded look was on his face again; a certain something that could not be accounted for by the extreme fatigue that she knew he must be experiencing.

'How do *you* know. . .?' she whispered, goaded by an inexplicable compulsion to know something more about him. 'Your daughter?'

He regarded her thoughtfully, as though weighing up the advisability of talking to her about much other than work. He was, it seemed, what was often called a very private person; not secretive necessarily, just very careful about who heard his confidences. She didn't blame him. There were really very few people who could be trusted with an intimate confidence; who would not judge.

'You don't have to answer that,' she said hastily. 'It's just that not many people are willing to put their money where their mouth is, so to speak.' She brushed her short, tousled hair back from her forehead. Perhaps he would unburden himself to her about his own child.

He smiled slightly, a smile of politeness this time.

'Are *you*, Miss Stewart?' he said perceptively, not answering her question.

'What. . .what do you mean?'

'I think maybe you prefer to sit on the fence. . .' he raised his eyebrows at her questioningly while she sat in silence, '. . .afraid to jump one way or the other. . . in case your decision should be wrong? Hmm?'

'I. . .I don't. . . How do you. . .?' she found herself stammering under the onslaught of his astuteness.

'Let's call it observation, based on experience. . . shall we?' he said, turning his attention back to his food, 'Eat up. . .it's all getting cold.'

Dutifully she began to eat, feeling chastened. Without seeming to try he had bared her unwilling soul.

'Am I right?' he said quietly, long minutes later, dominating her with his masculine presence, his will-power.

'Yes. . .I expect you are,' she said.

'Sometimes you have to have the guts to jump. . .one way or the other,' he said. 'To answer your original question, I had a wife and daughter once. Now I no longer have them.'

'Did you jump?' she asked, 'Do you?'

'Oh, yes. . .' he said.

'What. . .what is the next move for Mrs Ritter?' She took a large bite of a pancake to prevent herself from saying anything else inappropriate. They seemed to be talking in riddles; getting into deep water with danger-ous undercurrents.

'We'll know in the first two months whether her body's rejecting the liver, which is a possibility, in spite of the Cyclosporine she'll be taking every day. . .as you know.'

'Mmm. . .'

'Also, we'll know within that time if there's rejection for technical reasons. . .if I haven't done my job properly,' he said crisply. 'If she can remain rejection-free for one year the outlook is pretty good, although chronic rejection affects about five per cent of cases after that time. Cyclosporine has made a hell of a lot of difference to the success rate.'

Elaine knew that Cyclosporine itself was not without toxic side-effects. 'What are Carla Ritter's chances?' she said, thinking of the petite woman's frail body on the stretcher and of her fighting spirit.

'If we can get her over the next few days she has a pretty good chance,' he said. 'If I had thought otherwise I wouldn't have subjected her to such a traumatic operation. As you know, her condition was bad. We can already see that the liver's working so her body chemistry will gradually return to normal.'

For a while they ate in silence, acutely aware of his pager that rested silently on the table between them. It seemed to be a symbol of their separation somehow — a point beyond which she could not go. They finished the pancakes, then started on the melon and then the toast.

'I'll get us some more coffee.' Raoul Kenton stood up, as though aware of her discomfiture and her need for a small breathing space. 'Anything else you would like, Elaine?'

'No, thanks. This was just great. I really appreciate it.'

Now she wanted to leave as quickly as possible. Being with him had a bitter-sweet connotation. Sometimes she thought she might be falling in love with him, yet how unrealistic that state was, she thought. She was inexperienced, whereas he was sophisticated in such matters.

Somehow she must fight those feelings; be very professional. Before anything could hope to be lasting there had to be a friendship, a mutual support, a sure knowledge that a lasting, mature love would grow out of the 'in love' stage. 'Chemistry' was important, she mused as she watched him coming towards her again. . .and that chemistry was certainly there! Yet it was presumptuous in the extreme to think that he felt the same way. . .

'Thank you very much.' She forced herself to smile up at him as he handed her a mug of coffee. 'Your twenty minutes of uninterrupted time is just about up, I think.'

'Yeah. . .' He sat opposite her. 'I want to apologise for being somewhat boorish a few minutes ago. I'm a little sensitive still about my daughter. . .and my marriage. It's immature, I know.' He gave her a crooked, cynical grin that was coming to be familiar. 'Somewhat self-indulgent, too. Maybe one day I'll be over it.'

'It's all right.' She cupped her hands round the mug of hot coffee, lowering her eyes from his very perceptive gaze. 'I shouldn't have said anything. It has nothing to do with me.'

There was a silence, during which she did not look up.

'Are you planning to marry Matt Ferrera?' he asked softly.

Elaine looked up then, startled. 'No. . .no. . .of course not,' she blurted.

'Why ''of course''? It's not that self-evident. . .is it?' There was a quietness about him, an intensity as he looked at her as though he could see right through to her soul.

'It is to me,' she said, returning his look. 'Matt's a. . .' The sentence was never finished; an intermittent, shrill series of beeps from the gadget on the table between them made Elaine jump.

Raoul Kenton didn't turn a hair; just calmly switched it off.

'Right on cue,' he said wryly, picking it up and putting it into the pocket of his lab coat. They both smiled, commiserating. Then he swallowed the last few mouthfuls of his coffee as he stood up. 'Take care, Miss Stewart. See you in the operating room. . .but not too soon, I hope.'

Then he was striding away from her across the vast cafeteria, heading towards the internal telephone on the wall by the exit door and leaving her with a pounding heart, feeling churned up inside and decidedly confused by the mixed messages he appeared to be giving her.

'Oh, hell.' She let out a breath, willing herself to calm down. Absently she finished her coffee, her eyes on him helplessly as he made a telephone call. As though sensing her look he turned to give her a final salute before leaving the room.

The journey home later was going against the traffic, perhaps the only real bonus of working all night, Elaine acknowledged as she swung her small, compact car round the corner into her own street to park in front of the maroon-coloured door of the house where she had her flat. Reactions and reflexes were slow when you were exhausted, without reserves of energy. At least she had a pleasantly full stomach and could go to bed without having to prepare food. She was looking forward to a long day of sleep and rest, with Cornelius purring beside her.

Would she sleep? That question came to her as she tried unsuccessfully to push Raoul Kenton, who insisted on being just 'Raoul', from her mind. He seemed to be playing with her emotions, while being largely inaccessible himself.

CHAPTER SIX

LINDA OSTEY was transferred to a more general surgical unit at about the same time that Carla Ritter was taken off the critical list in the intensive care unit. It was evident that Linda, at least, would be home for Christmas. Angie Clark and Elaine made a quick visit to both of them before work one morning in December.

Carla, propped up in the bed that dwarfed her thin, petite body, was very pleased to see them. A lot of the puffiness and chronic tiredness was gone from her face.

'You don't know how precious your life is until you're faced with losing it,' she said when the preliminary greetings were over, past any false modesty or reticence about her feelings with them. 'I've had plenty of time to think about that, believe me. I'll never stop feeling grateful to all of you in whatever time I've got left. Just being able to see my kids smile again was worth all the pain.'

'You're a walking miracle, Carla,' Angie said jovially. 'At least, you will be in a day or two.'

'Oh, yes! They've had me up several times already. There's no slacking here.'

'It's great to see you looking so good, Carla,' Elaine added feelingly.

'Let me tell you. . .you don't realise how precious love is until you've had something like this operation. . . the people you love. . .the ones who love you. It gives you a whole new perspective. You sure get rid of all your old emotional baggage, believe me! There's not much that seems important after this. Just life and love. And you sure find out who your few really good friends

83

are. . .the ones who stand by you in trouble.'

Carla, her thin face animated, said those words as though she had been bottling them up, desperate to bring them forth to someone who would listen and understand. All the time that the ventilator had been breathing for her, with the endotracheal tube in her throat, she had not been able to speak. 'Nothing else matters much in the end,' she went on. 'You have to face up to saying goodbye to them if things don't turn out. . . Oh, the poignancy of it! I can't begin to tell you. . .'

Elaine gripped Carla's frail hand in silent commiseration. An image of a child she had never seen came to her mind. . . Raoul Kenton's child. In her mind's eye the child was as unusually fair as her father, with the same pale, tawny eyes—a wistful, sweet child. No wonder he had become withdrawn, closed in, shut off from any very involving contact, in spite of what he appeared to have with Dr Della Couts.

'Hang in there, Carla! We're all rooting for you. See you again later,' Angie said.

It was Dr Mike Richardson's day to operate; both Elaine and Cathy were working with him. Going through the familiar routine of work, Elaine found herself acutely missing Raoul. She tried his name out for size, saying the name over and over again silently in her mind. . . Raoul. . . Raoul. . . Raoul. It was an attractive name, she decided, a name that suited his uncommon attraction very well. She found herself counting the hours until she would see him again. Reluctantly she acknowledged that he would inevitably cause her pain.

'Drapes, please,' Dr Richardson asked. Silently she helped him to drape the patient from head to toe with disposable drapes, leaving only the operation site visible. It was to be an abdominal operation, a gut resection to remove a tumour. Matt Ferrera and Tony Asher joined them to be the assistant surgeons.

'Let's make a start then, Miss Stewart. Knife.'

It was a long, interesting operation that went calmly and smoothly without any unexpected happenings. In many ways it was very routine, although a big operation for the patient. With a gut resection there was very little bleeding as there were no really major blood vessels involved. Elaine liked these operations that went on for some time, where she could see clearly what was being done by the surgeon—something to really come to grips with rather than a lot of short, uninteresting procedures.

In between cases Matt turned his attention to Elaine. He crinkled up his warm, brown eyes at her in a smile. 'You're quiet today, Elaine,' he murmured, so that no one else could hear. 'Hormones acting up?' Matt had a wicked sense of humour, which he exercised at every opportunity.

'No!' Elaine said, emphatically. 'They're not acting up any more than yours are.'

'Tell me about it later.'

'Are you coming to the Christmas party with me?' Matt asked her later, just as their latest patient was being wheeled out of the room to be taken to the recovery room. 'You never did give me a proper answer. It's next Saturday.'

'Sure, Matt,' she said, trying to dredge up some enthusiasm. 'That would be great.' Up to now she had fantasised that Raoul might ask her to the dance; that he would hold her in his arms and move with her to the sound of slow, sensual music. As much as she liked Matt, she had wanted Raoul. Now she came down to earth. Wanting him might for ever remain in the realm of fantasy.

Matt was not blind to her antipathy. 'Let me remind you, kid,' he said, divesting himself of his soiled surgical gown, 'that I've got a couple of other possibilities at least, just panting to be asked by me to that dance.'

'I know, Matt,' she grinned. He wasn't joking. 'I won't be jealous if you spread yourself around.'

'I know you won't. That's the trouble,' he said meaningfully.

There was a line-up for lunch in the staff cafeteria. Mercifully it was moving quite quickly, an important factor when you had very little time for a lunch break. Elaine stood with her tray, waiting in line near the cash register.

'Hi, Elaine. How goes the struggle?'

Elaine turned to see Bill Radnor of the Multiple Organ Retrieval Service standing next to her. Bill was short and stocky, with a round, boyish face which belied his maturity and the great responsibility of his job. 'Hello, Bill. I'm pretty good,' she said.

She liked Bill; he was one-hundred-per-cent up front. Perhaps that was why he was able to do his job so well—because he brought to it a matter-of-factness that neither denied the seriousness and inherent sadness of the organ transplant service nor downplayed the importance of having living organs available. To him it seemed to be a matter of not throwing away something that could be used for a very good cause; just common sense really.

They sat together at a table and began to chat about Bill's over-riding passion, which was to go to the Rocky Mountains in western Canada to walk and climb and to get totally away from hospitals and death.

After a while she became aware that she was under scrutiny, had that odd feeling of a telepathic communication. As she moved her gaze to the left, away from Bill's eager face, she found herself looking into the intense eyes of Dr Kenton, seated a few tables away from them.

The expression on his face was absorbed and serious, as though he might have been watching her for some time. It was a guarded look, unreadable. Yet she instinctively, intuitively, recognised something in it that made her heart leap with a strange sense of shock, as though he had again touched her. As her cheeks warmed with an awareness of him she acknowledged that he was constantly on her mind now, not far from the surface.

Although Raoul did not operate on Thursdays he was, of course, in the hospital to see in-patients and to conduct his out-patient clinics in his private office. Tomorrow he would again be in the operating rooms with her. Elaine dragged her eyes away from him after giving him a brief acknowledging smile, then concentrated on stirring sugar into her coffee. What a mistake it was to breach the strict doctor/nurse relationship with someone like Raoul Kenton, she told herself furiously.

Matt Ferrera was different. As much as she liked Matt, it was a take-it-or-leave-it relationship; they had never been lovers. With Raoul, she knew intuitively again that it would only be a 'take it' situation from her point of view. If he were ever offering himself, that is.

'Do you think those two are going to get married?' Bill had stopped his account of mountain hiking and had followed her line of vision just as Dr Della Couts, carrying a glass of orange juice, joined Dr Kenton at his table. 'They seem to have something going for them. They sure make an attractive couple, if that's anything to go by. . .which I very much doubt.' Bill chuckled a little cynically.

'I. . .don't know either of them well enough to speculate. What do you think?' Elaine sipped her coffee, trying not to think of Raoul Kenton married to Della Couts. Somehow Dr Couts did not seem right for him. . . a little too hard, too brittle, or something.

If only she, Elaine, had not fainted; had not been held

and kissed by him. . .perhaps then she would not be as painfully aware of her medical colleague, would still be in blissful ignorance of him and her own responses.

'Well, I guess he'll be pretty careful next time around. If there is a next time,' Bill commented thoughtfully. 'His wife left him after their child died, so I heard from people who knew them. Then they divorced. I feel real sorry for the guy but I guess she couldn't hack it with him any more. . . They must have reminded each other all the time of the kid.'

'Where is she now? The wife?'

'Not with him. That's for sure,' Bill said succinctly. 'Anyway, to change the subject, when are you coming up to visit me again in my unit, Elaine? I've got some new printed material you ought to see. ''New and improved'', as they say. There's a new manual for the patients on the waiting lists to read—everything they need to know from A to Z.'

'Maybe next week some time, Bill.' Elaine remembered reading the information manual—compiled by the transplant programme co-ordinators—that had been required reading for her as part of her orientation program when she had first gone to work on the kidney transplant team. It had been put together for the patients who were on the waiting lists for donor organs to read.

'There are a few words in that manual, Bill, that have stuck in my mind from the first time I read them. Remember this? ''At a time of great suffering for them, the family of the donor have generously consented to the giving of an organ to you so that you may have a renewed opportunity for life and health.'' Hope that wording hasn't been changed.' She quoted the familiar words with deep feeling, conscious again of Dr Kenton looking over at her.

'It hasn't. I wrote that so I'm not about to see it

changed.' Bill smiled across at her, flattered by her appreciation. 'You see, Elaine, I have unsuspected abilities.'

'Yes, Bill, I do see.'

'I'll expect you some time next week, then.' Bill got up to leave and she followed suit in a few moments, feeling oddly exposed in that vast room with Dr Kenton only a short distance away, watching her, she thought, without appearing to do so. Why? That was the question. . .

'Elaine! Are you blind or something? As well as deaf? I've been calling you.' Matt Ferrera blocked her path just outside the cafeteria exit and he drew her aside by the arm out of the flow of people coming out. 'I want to fix a time to pick you up for the party.'

It struck her then that Matt was more like a brother than anything else. . .or perhaps a cousin. She could confide in him without fear that her confidence would be repeated to a third party. Matt draped a commiserating arm around her shoulders and brought his tousled head, with its black, curling hair, close to her own. He then planted a kiss on her cheek—in full view of Raoul Kenton and Della Couts as they came out of the cafeteria. 'Let me take you for a drink after work. OK?'

'Yes, OK,' she said a trifle defiantly as she found herself once again looking into the enigmatic eyes of Dr Kenton as he walked past them. His eyebrows had quirked slightly and there was now a glint of amusement on his face, as well as a touch of cynicism.

Deliberately she put her hand in the crook of Matt's arm as they walked towards the stairs that would take them up to the second floor of the Fraser wing and the operating rooms. What Dr Kenton perhaps did not know was that Matt distributed his casual kisses generously among the female staff.

At the edge of her vision she saw Raoul Kenton and Della Couts waiting for the elevators. Without actually looking, she registered that his head turned in her direction as she passed and she felt his eyes boring into the small of her back until she disappeared from his view.

'What time shall I pick you up on Saturday?' Matt prepared to leave her at the main entrance to the operating rooms.

'What. . .? Oh. . .about seven-thirty, Matt. Thanks. I'm looking forward to it.'

'You're not concentrating, are you? See you, kid!'

'Bye for now, Matt.'

At the end of Dr Richardson's operating list several hours later and when most of the clearing up had been done, Jill Parkes waylaid her again. 'Don't go home just yet, Elaine,' she said. 'I want to have a few words with you.'

'Oh, no!' Elaine said in mock horror. 'Not more bad news about Dr Kenton not wanting me on the team?'

'No, nothing like that,' Jill responded. Nonetheless, her face was thoughtful. Elaine held her tongue as one by one the other nurses in her unit called out their goodbyes.

'Get some beauty sleep, Elaine,' Angie called to her before going off duty, 'You're going to need it for that party Saturday. It's going to be real great, by the sound of it.'

'Bye, Angie,' she called back.

'Come into the prep room,' Jill said to her. When they were away from the busy rooms bordering onto the corridor, Jill turned to her. 'I've got good news and bad news. First of all the good news. Joe and I are thinking of getting married in a few weeks and maybe going out to Vancouver to live. What I want to ask you, Elaine, is whether you would be interested in taking my job as head nurse in Unit 2. You see, I've got a contract with the hospital which I'll have to cut short. The powers-that-be might not mind so much if I can recommend a replacement.'

'*Mamma mia*!' Elaine remarked, mimicking an exclamation that Matt commonly used. 'Well, congratulations! I had no idea. As for the job, Jill, I'm not sure that they would give it to me. Cathy's been in this unit longer. Does the co-ordinator know you're leaving?'

'No. I don't want to tell her until I've got someone interested in the job so they don't have to advertise for a replacement.' Jill busied herself shifting trays of sterile instruments about that were ready for the next operating day, while Elaine lounged against the stainless-steel counter where they sorted out their clean instruments at the end of the day, easing her feet out of her shoes.

'I think they'd be pretty interested in you, Elaine,' Jill went on. 'You've had more varied experience than Cathy. . .and I don't think she's particularly interested in being a head nurse here; she wants to travel. Angie said she wants to get married before she thinks of taking on more responsibility. I know you and Matt Ferrera aren't serious. . .are you?'

The casual question, sounding like a certainty, gave Elaine an odd stab of angst. 'No,' she agreed. 'You make me sound like a dedicated career woman, Jill. Do I come across like that?' Even as she forced a lightness to her tone she wanted to blurt out to Jill that it was Raoul Kenton who absorbed all her thoughts where the opposite sex was concerned.

'You're bloody good at your job, if that's what you mean. All the surgeons think you're great. Mike Richardson and Raoul Kenton, plus one or two of the other guys, would give you references any day, I'm sure, if I was to put your name forward for the job,' Jill said enthusiastically. 'What do you say?'

'Give me the weekend to think about it, Jill,' she said,

trying not to give anything away at the sound of Raoul's name. 'Which reminds me. . .' she glanced hastily at the wall clock '. . .Matt said he would take me for a drink after work. He'll be in here any minute, accusing me of hiding from him.' As she spoke, Raoul's words came back to her. . .something about sitting on the fence; having to have the guts to jump down. . . Taking a promotion would sure come into that category, she thought soberly.

'Sure.'

'What's the bad news?' she asked.

Jill stopped her activity, turning to face Elaine. 'I heard a little while ago that Carla's not so hot. Possible rejection.'

'Oh, no. . .no.' Elaine closed her eyes momentarily in anguish, the picture of Mrs Ritter's thin, pale face floating before her mind's eye. 'Oh, my God. I thought she was doing OK.'

'So did I. . .but apparently not,' Jill said quietly. 'The luck of the draw, eh?'

'Yes. . .' Elaine murmured distractedly, all thoughts of her personal life instantly wiped out of her mind.

'Since we're all on call this weekend stay close to home and near a telephone. I have a feeling we're going to be needed pretty quick if they decide to give her another liver. . .'

'They will, won't they? I mean. . .they won't just let her die?' Elaine blurted out. 'Dr Kenton wouldn't let that happen. . .?'

'No, of course not. It's a question of getting a suitable liver in time,' Jill said sombrely. 'You can be sure that Bill will be doing his best to get one. It won't be so difficult to get the failing liver out the second time around. . .but she could still bleed.'

They stood together in silence for a few minutes, each thinking of all the implications and their minds going over the necessary routine for them to be in an immediate state of readiness. 'Oh, Jill. . .' Elaine broke the silence, 'I could just weep.'

'Yeah, I know,' Jill said feelingly, her thin, prematurely mature face creased with anxiety. 'All we can do is be ready for the call. There's no potential donor in the hospital right now, apparently.'

'Her poor family. . .having to go through all that again.'

'Yeah. We'll just have to keep ourselves ready, that's all.' Jill repeated the words like a mantra as though they would, of themselves, keep their patient alive and the whole surgical team geared once again for a superlative effort in which the word 'failure' was never uttered.

CHAPTER SEVEN

'Do you care to dance with me, Miss Stewart? Or are you trying to avoid me like the proverbial plague? I did get that impression.'

There was a burst of laughter from the small group of people who stood together in the crowded and noisy ground-floor banqueting room of the MacKenzie Tower as Elaine pivoted on her high heels to focus on the speaker, tensing herself for the long-anticipated encounter. All evening she had waited for this; waited for him to notice her. . . Yet she had been fighting it at the same time.

The MacKenzie Tower was a twenty-two-storey building that had originally been built as a nurses' residence in more affluent days and where the annual medical and nursing staff Christmas party and dance was held each year. Conveniently, it was connected to the main part of the hospital by an underground tunnel.

Dr Kenton had made the drawling remark while his entourage turned, as though with one body, in her direction. The only person who did not laugh was Dr Della Couts, Elaine noticed distractedly from where she stood on the periphery of the group of 'liver people', as they were known in the hospital. Matt had deposited her there briefly at the end of a dance while he made a foray to the busy bar to get himself a drink. She had felt exposed there, tensely waiting yet wanting to be away from Matt.

All eyes in the group were suddenly on Elaine, including those of Raoul as he stood surveying her from several feet away—a distance that seemed like a chasm to her—where so many other people had a claim on him.

She was glad that she had worn a sophisticated black sleeveless sheath dress in a heavy crêpe that clung to the curves of her body naturally, showing her physical attributes without being too suggestive. Now she watched Raoul's eyes going over her blatantly as he withdrew a little from the group of his colleagues and moved indolently towards her. His gaze lingered on the swell of her breasts and then on the slender indentation of her waist and she was instantly aware of every quivering fibre in her body. The dress fell to just above her ankles in a slim line, with a slit at one side which showed more of her leg when she moved.

There might have been only the two of them in that festive room as he came to her. That vast space, loud with the sounds of music, conversation and laughter, receded for her in those few heart-stopping seconds in which he seemed to lay claim to her.

Wanting nothing more than to go into his arms, she nevertheless forced herself to remain on the spot. Refusing to be sycophantic or to display her nervousness, she did not join in the amusement. Her fingers gripped the long stem of her wine glass while the accelerated pounding of her heart somehow gave her courage. A small voice echoing in her brain warned her not to get involved and then was silent. . .

'I'm always on duty while I'm in the hospital, Dr Kenton,' she said, forcing a coolness that she did not feel, 'and I guess that dancing with you would come into the category of ''duty'', wouldn't it?'

Her tone belied the turmoil of her thoughts and the fact that she had been longing all evening to do just what he was suggesting. To that purpose she had found herself gravitating closer to him. If it became obvious there would be no end to the gossip that would surround them. There was laughter again from all those senior

people. To her he had never looked so attractive, dressed
in a formal black dinner jacket and bow tie.

When he took the wine glass from her fingers she
broke eye contact and seemed to come out of a
hypnotic state.

'You look very lovely, Elaine,' he said, his voice
husky and low this time so that no one else could hear.

'Thank you,' she murmured back. No doubt he had
already said that to Dr Couts, she thought frantically,
trying to bring a sobering cynicism into any contact
with him. She shivered as his warm fingers gripped her
bare upper arm. 'Come. I've been waiting for the good
Dr Ferrera to absent himself. I doubt that he'll be gone
for long.'

'Matt doesn't confine himself to me, Dr Kenton,' she
said. Indeed, that was true; Matt had been spreading
himself around rather thinly among the young female
population since their arrival at the party.

'I thought we had agreed that you would call me
Raoul,' he said, bending down to her attentively, his
tawny eyes alight with an awareness of her as an attractive woman. That knowledge started a deep, inner
trembling in her.

'It's not always easy for me to think of you that way,'
she protested, while feeling herself gravitate naturally
towards him. She allowed him to shepherd her towards
the area of the room that had a floor of polished wood
and had been designated as a dance floor.

She knew that she looked attractive. Wearing no
jewellery, she allowed the dress itself and the sophisticated high-heeled evening sandals that she wore, in a
fine black suede, to carry her appearance. Her hair, a
shining cap of burnished copper newly cut for the
occasion, completed the picture of slim sophistication.
If only he knew, she thought frantically, how primitive
her feelings really were. . .how easy it would be for him

to divest her of that protective veneer. . .

As though picked for the occasion, the band began to play a slow, sensuous number and at last. . .at long last. . . Raoul Kenton took her unresistingly into his arms. Their bodies touched and swayed in unison as his arm around her held her firmly against him while his other hand held hers warmly. 'Let yourself go,' he invited softly, his mouth against the sensitive lobe of her ear.

'Are you letting yourself go?' she asked challengingly, pulling back from him a little in the circle of his arms and raising her eyebrows at him questioningly.

'Sure!' he grinned down at her slowly in a way that made her heart flutter unpredictably and she lowered her eyes as he eased her close. There seemed to be a magic in the sensuous music, the festive lights. . .

Gradually relaxing against him and allowing herself to drift into the mood of the music, she gave herself up to the pure, longed-for delight of being in physical contact with him, wanting it to go on forever.

'Can you think of me as ''Raoul'' yet?' he murmured teasingly.

'I'm trying. . .' she said musingly. 'Give me a few more minutes.' She could feel him smile, feel his arm tightening around her, and she moved her hand on his shoulder so that her fingertips just touched the back of his neck, knowing instinctively that he was as acutely aware of her touch as she was of his. The knowledge brought a strange feeling of power and of humility at the same time. Her own vulnerability was almost complete.

'Will Matt Ferrera be looking for you?' he said. His hand slid down to her hips, holding her against him so that through the fabric of her dress she could feel the powerful muscles of his thighs as he moved with her.

'I. . .I don't think so. . . Matt has too many other interests.' All thoughts of Matt had gone from her mind.

'Good. . .' he said huskily, very close, his lips brush-
ing the corner of her waiting mouth. . .tempting her but
not taking her. Involuntarily she pressed herself against
him, unconsciously offering herself, even as the warning
voices clamoured in her mind. The wine she had drunk
sang in her veins, dulled her caution. . .

For dance after dance they stayed together, the music
of one blending into the next, without breaking contact.
Elaine felt her body tingling from head to toe with
awareness of him and she desperately wanted to move
her head the short distance so that they could kiss; it
took all her effort to prevent herself from doing it. If
only they were alone. . .

As the music died down the tinny sound of a beeper
penetrated their consciousness. Nonchalantly Raoul
reached into his pocket to switch it off. 'I have to call
Locating,' he said, capturing her hand again. 'Come
with me.'

Quickly they picked their way to the edge of the dance
floor through the crush of couples. Elaine followed him,
teetering on her high heels, very aware of the enveloping
warmth of his hand covering hers. They were heading
for the corridor beside the banqueting hall where they
would find a telephone to call Locating, the service that
was responsible for finding all staff at all times.

'Thank God for Locating,' she murmured lightly as
she hurried to keep up with him, hoping that he was not
about to be taken away from her by hospital demands.

Near the door of the semi-dark room, which was
festooned with streamers and coloured balloons, Raoul
paused, pulling her up against him. 'Look up there,'
he said.

Obediently she looked up. Hanging from the high
ceiling, on a very long ribbon, was a huge bunch
of mistletoe, partially hidden behind an unlighted
Christmas tree. 'Mmm. . .' she murmured her appreci-

ation provocatively, invitingly. 'It's plastic, I think. Does that matter?'

'No,' he answered her thickly. Suddenly the air between them was electric with the unspoken desire that had been building between them as they had danced. Elaine no longer questioned it; merely accepted it. More than anything she wanted to kiss him and knew that it showed in her eyes as she looked at him. The bunch of fake mistletoe somehow gave them permission—the final impetus.

Behind the shelter of the tree they went into each other's arms with frantic haste, while the booming music of a frenetic rock number crashed around them and coloured lights flickered crazily around the room as the tempo of the party increased a few notches.

With her arms around his neck Elaine lifted her face to his, parting her lips in expectation and pressing her body frantically against his. They only had moments to spare—precious, treasured moments—before the call to duty had to be answered.

The kiss was very different from the kiss he had given her in her kitchen, the kiss of comfort. Now he crushed her mouth with his; enveloped her in his arms as though he was starved for the touch of a woman. And she responded with all the fervour of her being. . .with all the weeks of frustrated longing. . .and with all the poignant tenderness that she felt for him when she thought of his lost child and that she could not put into words.

Her hands moved to his hair, her fingers stroking and twining in its thickness as she stood on tiptoe to press herself against him, wanting to melt into him so that they could be one body, one mind. His mouth moved on hers, demanding, dominating, exploring. . .leaving her in no doubt that he wanted her sexually, was as moved by her as she was by him.

His fierce need both frightened and exhilarated her.
Here was no mere boy, no tentative lover; Raoul Kenton
was one-hundred-per-cent mature man. How she longed
then to meet the challenge of him completely as she
tremblingly responded to him.

'Oh, Raoul. . .' His name was dragged from her as
he momentarily took his mouth from hers to kiss her
neck and then her bare shoulder where the dress fell
away; as he ran his hands over her body where the crêpe
of her dress moulded to her like a second skin.

Then he savagely took her mouth again, insinuating
his tongue between her soft lips and leaving her in no
doubt that he wanted her desperately; he hugged her
against him, his strong arms encircling her possessively.
She responded mindlessly, feeling herself swept away
by an uncontrollable tide of passion that she had not
known could exist between a man and and a woman—
had only guessed at.

'Does this come into the category of duty?' he said
at last, raising his voice against the music, having taken
his mouth from hers to nuzzle the side of her neck.
Like her own, his breathing came in unsteady, trembling
gasps that betrayed his need.

'No!' She laughed breathlessly, her head thrown back
so that he could kiss her exposed throat. 'I'm not sure
what category this comes into.'

The persistent beeping broke through the spell of their
mutual passion that had all the power of a narcotic
drug. Languidly, reluctantly, they drew apart, hands still
clinging, touching. . .

'Damn!' he said, 'I'll have to answer it.'

Hand in hand they emerged into the harsh fluorescent
light of the corridor, blinking against it, and set a brisk
pace towards the public telephones and the internal telephones that were reserved for the use of doctors and
nurses on call and on duty.

Elaine stood beside him as he punched in a number. Delirious with an unprecedented happiness, she was living for the moment and not daring to think beyond it, only knowing that she wanted nothing more than to be back in Raoul Kenton's arms and to feel his demanding mouth on hers.

'Hi, Bill,' he said, at length, on the second ring, 'What's up?'

Those few words had a chilling effect on Elaine as she stood beside Raoul at the telephone—like the proverbial bucket of cold water. It was obvious that he was talking to Bill Radnor of the MOR Service. . .and that could only mean one thing. The question was, would it mean now. . .or later?

She moistened her swollen lips with the tip of her tongue, hardly daring to breathe as she strained to hear. Raoul, who was saying very little, just listened intently to what Bill was saying. As he listened Elaine watched him at close quarters. She let her eyes move over his features—his chiselled mouth that had crushed hers moments before, his firm jaw-line, his pale hair that hung so attractively just above his collar. Just as she longed to touch him again she knew that for now the opportunity was over.

'OK, Bill,' he was saying now, 'that's great! Sure. . . sure. We might as well get on with it.'

When he finished the conversation he turned to Elaine, confirming what she had suspected. 'Bill's found a liver for Carla; it's a good match. We'll operate tonight as soon as it gets here. It's coming from the States. Unfortunately the other one is being rejected; the sooner we can get it out the better.' His eyes had that intent, preoccupied look of a man gearing up for work once again after a brief respite.

'Yes. . .' she agreed. 'Most of the team is here, I think.' She felt empathy for him; he seldom seemed to get more than a few minutes to himself. Maybe that was why his wife had chosen not to live with him. . .

'I'll get the music stopped in there while I make an announcement to round up the team. . .and I've got to talk to Dr Couts. We've got about two hours before the liver gets here,' he said. 'Look. . . Elaine. . .why don't you go straight over to the OR? The others can join you later. . .'

He reached forward to put his hand on the side of her neck in a brief caressing gesture that was oddly intimate and she felt a lump of emotion rise in her throat. 'Sorry I couldn't give you more notice. . .sorry it had to be right at this moment. But that's the luck of the draw.' His words seemed to imply much.

There was so much she wanted to say to him yet such words would be inappropriate now. Perhaps she would never get to utter them. 'Thanks for the dances,' she said as brightly as she could, smiling at him ruefully. 'I was just beginning to enjoy myself. I. . .guess that work is more our style.' She began to back away from him. 'See you in the OR.'

'Yeah. . .' he said, returning her smile. He seemed about to add something else but she turned impulsively from him and began to walk away as fast as her fitted dress and high-heeled shoes would allow, aware that her hips were undulating unnaturally as she moved and that her whole body swayed provocatively. She was also aware that he stood watching her until she had disappeared from his view down a flight of stairs that would take her to the connecting underground tunnel to the main hospital building, from where she could get an elevator to the OR locker rooms.

Down in the tunnel, where there were hissing steam pipes and gurgling water pipes, she made good progress, striding out determinedly as fast as her shoes would allow. Mingled emotions vied for precedence; there was regret at the cutting short of that devastating kiss and there was a sobering fear for the fate of Carla Ritter, who must once again face the terrible ordeal of her life on the line. Would she come out of it alive? The situation was critical.

Elaine tried not to think about that as she walked. She concentrated instead on the step-by-step procedure that she would set in motion as soon as she was changed into her scrub suit in the OR. Hard on her heels would be the other members of the team.

There was an atmosphere of determined, dedicated concentration that was touched with a certain frantic quality as Carla Ritter was finally wheeled into the operating room in Unit 2 for the second time.

Elaine barely glanced at the pale face of their patient; looked just long enough to register her arrival before transferring her attention once again to the instruments on her set-up that she had been counting with Cathy Stravinsky. Feeling sick at heart, she was determined that from her angle nothing would go wrong.

'I've got ten needle-holders,' she said, 'and twenty packets of sutures.'

'OK.' Cathy wrote down the numbers. 'Is that the lot?'

'Yep, that's it,' she said calmly, her tone belying her inner apprehension. They all felt it. . .the overlying silence engendered by an uncertain outcome. 'I'm all set.'

'Cheer up,' Cathy hissed at her. 'One thing you can be sure of—you look absolutely gorgeous! We all do. I haven't seen such a heavily made-up female liver crew since the last Christmas party. That green eye-shadow sure looks good on you.'

'Thanks, that's a great help!' Elaine hissed back with mock sarcasm. 'We go well together then, since you're smelling like the perfume counter at a department store.'

'Better than the usual scent of sweat and iodine, eh?' Cathy grinned before moving away to help Jill with their patient, prior to the giving of the anaesthetic.

'Sure!' Elaine confirmed, allowing herself to relax a bit now that she was ready. For some time now she had been scrubbed, getting her sterile set-up ready. Glancing at the clock, she saw that it was exactly two and a half hours since she had stood with Raoul at the telephone.

When he came into the operating room he came straight over to her. 'This won't take anywhere near as long as it did the first time around,' he said, his attitude very professional now. 'For one thing there won't be as much scarring or so many adhesions as there were surrounding Carla's own liver. And hopefully she won't bleed so much. . . We've got some of that under control.'

'Good,' she said. 'I'm ready.' She did not ask what Carla Ritter's chances were and he did not volunteer an opinion. Yet the question hung in the air like a tangible thing; it was even more evident as the other members of the surgical team filed silently into the room from the scrub sinks. The anaesthetist went quietly and efficiently about his work.

Soberly she helped the team into their sterile gowns and gloves. There were no jokes this time—no light-hearted quips. Perhaps the difference between the raucous noise of the party that they had just left and this life-and-death scene highlighted some of the bizarre contrasts that made up their lives. Work hard and play hard; that was their motto. If you didn't play hard occasionally, you went under.

'Ready for the prep, Elaine?' Raoul asked her.

'Yes.'

'OK to prep, Claude?'

'Yep. Go right ahead.'

*   *   *

There was seldom a thirteenth floor in high-rise buildings, Elaine reflected inconsequentially as the elevator sped upwards in the MacKenzie Tower; the numbering went from twelve to fourteen. It was odd, she thought, that in the high-tech world in which they moved such old superstition should still prevail.

At the fourteenth floor she got out, stepping with her high-heeled shoes onto the deep plush carpet of the corridor that led to the various rooms on either side and round corners in either direction. Taking off her shoes, she began to pad along, enjoying the feel of the carpet on her bare feet. From her hands a key swung on a chain. This was the floor where the liver team slept overnight if necessary. All was quiet.

Rounding a corner of the corridor silently, she came face to face with Raoul Kenton as he was about to enter one of the rooms there and her mouth formed itself into a silent 'O' of surprise at the sight of him.

'Hi,' he said quietly, the first to recover. 'It looks like the whole team's here. Let's hope we won't be required to do anything more.'

'Yes. . .I hope so too.'

There was a moment of awkwardness as his eyes went over her from head to bare feet; as the memory of their embrace flooded back. Elaine clutched her winter coat around her that covered the evening dress she had decided to put back on after her shower in the nurses' locker room at the end of the successful operation. She carried a bag containing the jeans and sweatshirt that she always kept in her locker for such emergencies.

The incongruity of her attire suddenly struck them as funny at the same time and they both smiled, while Elaine felt her face reddening.

'Where are you going to be?' he asked. He wore a clean scrub suit and lab coat that did not disguise his muscular, athletic frame. There was a stubble of beard on his pale face.

'Room twenty-seven,' she said, consulting the tab off the key once again, 'which I believe is right next to you.'

'Yes, it is,' he confirmed. 'Would you like to come in for a glass of cognac? I think we need it after that ordeal, don't you?'

There was a tenseness between them that sent warning bells clamouring through Elaine's mind, even as every fibre of her being longed to grasp his invitation. There was a depression, too, about the outcome for their patient.

'We won't talk shop,' he said soberly. 'Everything that there is to say about Mrs Ritter has already been said. Now we can only wait.'

'Yes. . .' Elaine agreed. Sufficient for now was that Carla Ritter had survived the operation, which had taken only half the time of the original. There were enough hours left of the night that they could hope to sleep while the night staff took over. The image of their patient's face would be with her for a long time.

Elaine bit her lip indecisively and ran a hand through her hair. Instinctively she knew that it would not be wise to accept his invitation. . .not while that sense of unfinished business weighed so heavily upon her so that she felt somehow she was having difficulty breathing when she looked at him.

'I don't know about you,' Raoul said lightly, deftly unlocking the door to his room, 'but I know I won't be able to sleep for quite a while. . .tired though I am. I doubt that you'll be any different.'

To her surprise, she realised that he was trying to persuade her and the thought was flattering as well as exciting. . .he actually wanted her company. Then she knew that she very definitely wanted his.

'You're probably right,' she said, trying to sound

casual. 'I would love a drink. . .thank you.'

The first thing that caught her attention when he switched on a table lamp in the room was the large bed that was pushed against a wall. The whole room and its furnishings were more luxurious, befitting the head of the surgical team, than the cell-like room with a shared bathroom that she would be occupying. A soft glow of light added a cosiness to the surroundings that would still have seemed somewhat utilitarian in daylight.

'Take your coat off. Make yourself comfortable,' Raoul invited, his voice deep and casual as he slipped out of his lab coat and flung it over a chair as though he was glad to get rid of it.

Somewhat self-consciously Elaine took off her coat and deposited her bag on the floor. 'I can't stay long,' she said. 'Any minute now I think I may crash out.'

'So long as you don't faint I think I can cope with that,' he said, smiling at her. Although his face showed his fatigue he was surprisingly alert and relaxed. It occurred to her then that he was slowly seducing her. . . and she was not sure that she minded. Once again she seemed to be coming alive in his presence; coming back to herself. . .and her heart began to pound with a new accelerated beat. Events seemed to take on a life of their own.

'What will you be doing for Christmas?' he asked, turning from his task of pouring drinks to look at her as she stood in the centre of the small room in her long, clinging evening dress. That look belied the prosaic question; it assessed her potential as a woman.

'Um. . .' She cleared her throat. 'I'll be with my parents at their place and my sister. . . Joanne. . .she'll be coming up from the States to join us. She's working down there—in Texas.'

'And what does she do?' he asked, coming towards her with two drinks in brandy balloons. Elaine found herself steeling her body against the effect of his closeness. It was useless.

'She. . .she's a doctor—an anaesthetist.'

'Really!' he said, raising his eyebrows at her as he handed her the drink. 'Did you ever want to do medicine?'

'No. . .I didn't.' She took the glass from him and their fingers touched, sending a wave of heat through her. 'I always felt that nursing was more "hands on". . .that was what I wanted. Also, I didn't want to seem to be competing with Joanne. She's four years older than I am and my parents were so proud of her. . .long before I even knew what I wanted to do with my life. They talked about her ad nauseam. . .so I chose nursing.'

'Are they proud of you?' he asked softly, almost tenderly, looking at her very astutely with his tawny eyes that seemed to miss nothing, 'or did they make you feel second-best?'

Elaine took a tiny sip of the cognac, holding it in her mouth for a few moments before swallowing. 'I know that they're proud of me. . .now. It's just that there's no younger sibling for them to boast to about me.'

'They should be proud of you,' he murmured. They were standing close and, as though mesmerised, she watched him raise his glass to his lips, remembering how those lips had ravaged hers. 'And what are your hopes for the future?'

'Oh. . .I want to continue what I'm doing with my work. One day I hope to get married. . .have children,' she said unthinkingly, musingly, before pulling herself up short, sensing that marriage was a tricky subject to be talking about with him. 'Anyway. . .' she paused to sip her own drink '. . .is this some sort of inquisition?' she added teasingly.

'You intrigue me,' he said.

'What will you be doing for Christmas?' she asked,

getting away from dangerous ground, feeling the absurdity of making conversation when what they both wanted to do was go into each other's arms. Unwittingly he had tapped into her adolescent angst about the future, still unchanged.

'Working, probably,' he said, his voice expressionless.

'I mean. . .where will you have your Christmas dinner? To me, that's a big part of Christmas.'

'I usually go to a hotel,' he said, looking at her with a cynical expression. 'First class, of course. Does that appall you, little Miss Stewart?'

'No. . .it saddens me,' she said, truthfully. 'Don't laugh at me because that's what I like.'

'Christmas is for children—for families,' he said brusquely. 'Since I have neither I like to get it over with as quickly and simply as possible.'

'Oh, Raoul. . .you're so adamant. . .' she said softly, the words dragged from her, 'as though there's nothing more to be said. Don't be so bitter. . .'

'Why not? I *am* bitter.'

'Raoul. . .perhaps you should try to make a new start,' she dared to say, given courage by the drink that was warming her body. 'I know this may sound gauche to you. . .but perhaps it's time that you said yes to life. That's what our patients are doing. . .when they consent to the operations we do on them. . .'

They were both still standing very close, so that she could watch the play of emotion on his face. 'And are you intending to help me to say yes to life?' he said softly, dangerously.

Before she could think of a reply he leaned forward across the short space between them and placed his mouth on hers, barely touching; she could taste the cognac on his lips and smell it on his breath. Without touching her anywhere else and connected only by their touching mouths, he began to move his lips gently on hers, teasing her. . .so that she stood paralysed with an uncommon delight.

Then she felt the tip of his tongue delicately outlining her lips and she felt her eyes languidly close under the almost imperceptible onslaught. When she felt his tongue move between her parted lips she felt a sharp stab of desire deep within her body and she knew that she had no power to resist him.

It took her a few seconds to understand that the small moan that she heard had escaped from her—a sound of longing, deep within her throat. She stood with eyes closed as he took her glass from her hand; she heard him place it on the bedside table and then he was with her again.

He held her lightly around the waist and she felt his other hand on her breast, the palm flattening and caressing her soft, sensitive flesh until she gasped with pleasure.

'Raoul. . .' at last she found her voice and opened her eyes '. . .I don't think we should be doing this. . .'

'Why not?' he murmured, his lips now caressing her cheek. When he pulled back to look at her she felt a deep sense of shock at the naked desire, the need, on his face. 'I'm saying yes to life. . . Do you mind?'

All she could think of at that moment was Dr Della Couts. What was his relationship with her that he now showed such obvious sexual need? Surely they were lovers. . .surely? As his eyes bored into hers she knew that she was lost—that he must be reading her as easily as she was reading him.

She moistened her lips in an unconsciously provocative gesture, so that his eyes moved to her mouth. 'No. . .' she whispered, deciding to be perfectly honest, 'I don't mind. Please. . .kiss me.'

With his hands on her breasts, moving tantalisingly,

he looked down at her. 'Mmm. . .' he said appreciatively, his voice low with a vibrating emotion, 'I have every intention of kissing you.'

Then there was no pretence. As though in slow motion she put her arms around his neck and he brought his head down to hers and covered her mouth possessively with his, seeming to draw her into him as though he wanted to devour her again. When her tongue met his in a sensuous parody of love-making she lost all sense of time and place and responded helplessly to the primitive sound of reciprocated pleasure that he made deep within his throat.

She made no protest when she felt his hands on the cleverly concealed zip of her very expensive dress and felt the cool air of the room play on her skin as he drew it down. The kiss only deepened when at last his warm hands touched the bare skin of her back. . .and then, at long last, her naked breasts. . .

CHAPTER EIGHT

'ARE you all right, Elaine?' Angie Clark waylaid her in the clean prep room on the Monday morning after they had finished their first case of the day. 'You look absolutely awful. . .and I do mean awful!'

'Thanks, Angie!' Elaine said sarcastically, hoping that her sarcasm would hide the terrible hurt that was consuming her. 'With you as a friend who needs enemies. . .as they say. I didn't sleep much over the weekend, if you must know. First there was the transplant and then there was. . .something else. Don't question me about it now.'

Deftly she opened the door of the small autoclave in which she had sterilised a few extra instruments for the next case on the operating list. Not looking at her friend, not wanting to confront her perceptive eyes, she lifted the sterile instrument tray out with a special forcep designed for the purpose. 'Make way,' she said.

Not easily put off, Angie followed her into the operating room where she deposited the tray on a sterile set-up. They were between cases. Cathy Stravinsky, who was to be the scrub nurse for the next case with Raoul Kenton, was having a quick coffee-break. Everything there had to be 'quick', Elaine thought ruefully as she cried inside, outwardly going about her usual business.

'Is it something to do with Raoul Kenton?' Angie made an educated guess. 'You were sure dancing with him a lot at the party on Saturday before that call. Want to talk about it?'

'Not now!' she said emphatically, her voice breaking

as her iron control slipped a little. 'I expect it's just me being hypersensitive or something. Or maybe I just expect too much. . .I don't know, Angie. Maybe one just shouldn't expect anything. It's safer that way.'

'Then it is him!' Angie breathed, her curiosity obviously piqued. 'Sounds bad to me. Has he been a bastard to you or something?'

Just then Cathy Stravinsky came back into the room. 'OK if I get scrubbed?' she asked.

'Sure, go ahead,' Angie answered her, covering up for Elaine who seemed to have momentarily lost her voice. 'Elaine's going for her coffee-break now.'

When they were alone again Angie confronted her friend. 'How about coming over to my place after work for supper and a glass or two of wine? You can get this all off your chest. OK? I owe you one.'

'Thanks, Angie,' Elaine said dully. 'Yes, I'd like that.'

She must have been the last nurse to take a coffee-break, she thought as she poured herself coffee moments later in the vacant nurses' coffee-lounge. Her mind inevitably went back to that awful scene she had had with Raoul Kenton on the Saturday evening. Why had she been such an idiot to fall for him so readily? To let him make love to her. . .?

No, it had not been quite like that—she had been a very willing participant in the end. Oh, God. She groaned out loud. Her own behaviour had been a revelation to her—the depth of her own passion, her willing abandon—as had been the totality of his response. He had not hesitated to take all that she had to offer; had seduced her in every sense of that word.

Without knowing quite how it had happened, light-headed with fatigue and the cognac she had drunk that Saturday night, she had found herself on the wide bed in his room, her dress a heap on the floor beside it.

Her arms, as though of their own volition, had reached for him as he had lowered himself down beside her on the bed. He had removed the top half of his loose cotton scrub suit, revealing his broad, naked torso. Delightedly, she had smoothed her hands over him, pulling him to her as he had gathered her in his arms.

When, moments later, she had felt his hand on her thighs, caressing her in such a way that she could have no doubt that he intended to make love to her, she had not protested. Every fibre of her being had welcomed him. It had taken him only moments to divest her of what remained of her clothing and then they had matched each other in a terrible, hungry need. . .a passion that had left no room for anything else. . .

One thing she did remember with certainty was that he had taken care to protect her against pregnancy and possible disease. Now the efficiency of that manoeuvre raised all sorts of other questions in her mind, grateful though she had been at the time.

It had all been so perfect, so devastatingly wonderful. . .until the telephone had rung as they'd lain side by side in the aftermath of their love-making.

'Hello, Dr Kenton here,' he said, having got up to walk a few paces to a desk to pick up the receiver. At the time she lay as though frozen in one spot, marvelling at his ability to sound calm, as though he had just woken from a sleep. Then, 'Hi, Dell,' he said. 'How's it going?'

She, Elaine, was horrified then, knowing that he was talking to Dr Couts and wondering if his colleague would want to come to his room to talk to him in person. Such thoughts brought her quickly back to earth.

The two doctors talked for some time, obviously about Mrs Ritter, who was being taken care of in the post-op period by Dr Couts. Raoul did most of the listening, only asking very pertinent questions. During that conversation Elaine got quietly off the bed, groped around for her underwear and got dressed, including the donning of her coat.

It was what happened afterwards that was so awful. At the end of the conversation he came over to her where she was sitting indecisively on the edge of the bed. The lower half of his body was wrapped with a towel, a makeshift garment that he wore casually, as though it were everyday attire for him. Her vulnerability must have been very clear on her face then as she was unable to take her eyes off him.

After looking at her for a long moment, he said, 'You were right when you said we shouldn't be doing this.' Those words, sounding so logical, were like a slap in the face to her. Had she said that? Yes, she recalled the words. . .they seemed to have been uttered a very long time before.

'It's very convenient to say that now,' she blurted out hotly. 'Now that. . .it's happened. Why do you say that now?'

'It could be. . .very awkward. . .for both of us,' he said slowly, having sat down heavily beside her.

'I'm not going to talk about it to anyone else. . .if that's what you mean; I can keep a confidence,' she said practically, feeling as though she was dying inside, her emotions a frazzled jumble. 'I. . .don't regret what happened even if you do. And you. . .you obviously wanted me.'

'Yes, I did,' he murmured. 'That doesn't mean it was wise. I apologise, Elaine, since I was the one to take the initiative. It won't happen again.'

'You don't have to apologise,' she said, standing up. Her whole being was protesting against his obvious rejection of her—no less a rejection because it was couched in practical terms. 'I'm not some sort of virginal maiden that you have to apologise to.'

'Nonetheless, I apologise if it seemed calculated,'

he said tiredly, standing up beside her.

'I'm intrigued. . .to see how you do it,' she said, wanting to hurt him as he was hurting her with his cool assessment—like the proverbial knife twisting in her heart. 'You make love to a woman and then apologise to make sure it will never happen again. Is that how you get rid of them, Dr Kenton?'

'No, it isn't,' he said wearily. 'I have no current sexual partner.'

'Not. . . Dr Couts?'

'No. Even a workaholic like me breaks out sometimes.' His haggard face was cynical with self-mockery. 'You're an attractive, intelligent, likeable woman. I enjoyed making love to you, Elaine. But I don't want to hurt you. . .which I might do.'

'Why?'

'After my marriage was over I vowed never to get as deeply involved with a woman again. So far, I've succeeded. . .and found a measure of contentment.' His voice sounded flat and Elaine felt a flood of compassion for him that over-rode her deep hurt.

'You can't hide forever, Raoul,' she said quietly. It would have been dishonest to pretend that she wouldn't like to get involved with him so she didn't even try. 'You're still a young man. Will you feel the same when you're forty-five? Fifty?'

He shrugged. 'Who knows? I live from month to month, from year to year. And I'm not exactly hiding, as you put it. My life is as full as I want it to be at the moment. My love is my work. My work is my life.'

There seemed no more to be said then, even though her whole being was crying out to touch him and begging to stay with him. As she turned away she saw for the first time a small framed photograph of a child on the bedside table. It appeared to be an ordinary snapshot of a child in a garden on a summer day—a little fair-haired girl smiling up at the camera and squinting against the sun.

'You must have been a good father,' she said quietly and spontaneously, turning to look at him, moved beyond endurance by the sight of the child. 'You could be again. Goodnight. . . Raoul.'

Quickly she made her exit, jerking open the door clumsily as tears started in her eyes. The door clicked shut behind her as she emerged into the silent corridor, signifying her exclusion from his life. No doubt she was not the first woman who had tried to break through the barriers he had put up. With tears smarting in her eyes, she realised that he had shut her out in every sense of the word. . .and the awful thing was she was pretty sure that in the height of their love-making she had whispered that she loved him.

Was that true? she asked herself despairingly. What a fool she was to be so obvious. Not sure of anything any more, except the terrible ache in her heart, she wanted the sanctuary of her own room. Then, in that small room, without putting on a light, she cried silently, standing against the door. What hope had she against his entrenched grief and his vow never to experience that again?

Now, back at work on the Monday morning and working with him again, he appeared exactly the same to her superficially. He was his same calm, courteous, co-operative self, always charming to the staff in a played-down way. Yet, hypersensitive to him now in a new way, she sensed in him a deeper withdrawal.

'I thought you'd decided to go for lunch too,' Angie said to her when she entered the operating room in her unit, looking meaningfully at the clock.

'Sorry,' Elaine said shortly, 'I decided to put on a bit of make-up since you were kind enough to inform me that I looked particularly awful.'

'OK, OK,' Angie capitulated. 'Just joking. Every-thing's quiet here. You want to scrub for the next case?'

'No,' she said hastily, 'I'd rather keep my distance today, if you don't mind.'

'Sure.'

The day moved briskly from then on as each com-pleted case was followed smoothly by the next. Elaine spent the day as the 'circulating nurse', while Jill Parkes supervised all four operating rooms in Unit 2. Deftly Elaine avoided close proximity with Raoul, although she was forced to tie up his surgical gown after he had scrubbed for each case which was part of her job. Each time he murmured his thanks in the usual manner. When he looked at her she did not meet his glance.

When they were just about to start the last case of the day she finally broke silence with the question that had been burning to be asked all day: 'How is Mrs Ritter, Dr Kenton? I haven't managed to get to see her yet.'

In truth she had been apprehensive about seeing Carla; had needed time to psych herself up before con-fronting the sight of the very ill woman fighting for her life. The words that Carla had uttered after the last operation—'You don't know how precious your life is until you're faced with losing it'—haunted her.

'So far, so good,' he said. 'She's holding her own. The liver function tests look good. No obvious rejection yet. Her family's there with her most of the time, which is what she wants. A very brave woman.'

Elaine was forced to look at him briefly then and to turn her haunted eyes with their swollen lids on him for a moment. She saw his eyes narrow perceptively, a question in them as he subtly took in her appearance. No doubt he had noticed the difference in her first thing that morning. Well, she wasn't going to give him the satisfaction of confirming in any way that he was responsible for the signs of grief on her face. He was no fool yet she would do what she had to do to keep him guessing; to salvage some shreds of her tattered pride.

Matt cornered her, too, after their last patient was wheeled out of the room to go to the recovery room. 'What's wrong with your eyes?' he said, getting straight to the point in his usual unsubtle way. 'They look pretty swollen to me.'

'Must be some sort of allergy,' she countered. 'I was sneezing a lot over the weekend too.'

'What, allergies at this time of the year? Allergic to what?'

'Who knows? City pollution maybe,' she said, moving away from his curious stare. 'Or maybe I'm just allergic to you.'

'Yeah. . .I often wonder,' he agreed. 'Well, take care, kid. See ya!' To her relief he disappeared from the room, taking the patient's chart with him.

'Let's get out of here as fast as we can,' Angie said in an undertone. 'I want to get you sorted out. . .before anyone else comments on your allergies! Is supper still on for us at my place?'

'Yes. . .please, Angie. I'm looking forward to it. Just want to dash up quickly to see Carla.'

Just as she was leaving for the day, having agreed to meet Angie in the locker room, Jill Parkes hurried up to her. 'Elaine, have you thought any more about what I asked you about taking over my job? I've got to speak to the co-ordinator any day now; have to think about giving in my notice.'

'I can't imagine this place without you, Jill,' she said truthfully. 'You hold this place together. I can imagine it all degenerating into chaos.'

'Nice of you to say so,' Jill replied modestly. 'You could do the same. I would teach you the ropes before I leave, of course.'

'I have thought about it,' Elaine said, pausing and taking a deep breath before plunging in. 'I was wondering if you could ask if I could be acting head for, say, three months and then apply for the job after that if I wanted to. You see. . .I'm not one-hundred-per-cent sure that I want the job. . .I think I do right now but the reality of the responsibility may be entirely different.'

What she could not say to Jill was that she felt as though she would be cutting herself off from the possibility of marriage if she took the job. . .there would be so little time for anything else other than work. At the same time the taunting words that Raoul Kenton had uttered about her 'sitting on the fence', afraid to jump either way, were in the forefront of her mind.

Jill must have read her thoughts. 'I understand how you feel,' she said instantly. 'I know exactly. What worked for me was that I decided I'd do the job for a set time and then quit if I found it all-consuming. That's exactly what I've done. The experience looks good on a résumé and I can get another head nurse job in a less busy place if I want to.' Then she added, with admirable candour, 'Look at me. . .I'm getting married. The job hasn't taken me out of circulation entirely. True, I did know Joe before I agreed to take it.'

The need to confide in Jill about Raoul Kenton was very strong, yet Elaine decided to say nothing. When the man she was getting involved with was in the same place what did it matter really whether she took a more responsible job or not. . .when that man was very unlikely to propose marriage to her. . .or anything else permanent? He certainly didn't sit on any fence, as he had intimated; he had already decided that for him a permanent woman was out!

'I'll take it temporarily, Jill, if they'll let me. Play it by ear, so to speak.'

'Thanks, that's great. I'll see what I can do. I know

they'll prefer to make an internal promotion rather than advertise outside.'

Before heading for the locker rooms she hurried to the intensive care unit, feeling compelled to at least see their transplant patient, although she did not want to intrude on the privacy of the family.

It was too late to veer away when she saw that Raoul was in Mrs Ritter's room; he was talking to her husband. Without his operating mask and cap Raoul looked unusually tired and strained, Elaine noticed with a jolt of compassion. Had he perhaps been more affected by what had taken place between them on the Saturday night than he had admitted? There was a tense set to his mouth, a rare air of distraction about him. Perhaps she was flattering herself if she thought his looks had anything to do with her, she thought cynically as she advanced into the room to talk to the nurse.

'Hi,' the nurse greeted her quietly. 'Better luck the second time around, eh?' They exchanged commiserating smiles. 'She's doing OK; we can't complain.'

'Good, I'm so glad,' Elaine said feelingly.

Not wanting to intrude, she could see from a distance that Carla was asleep, her pale face turned to one side on the pillow. Although she looked worn out from her ordeal she also looked very much alive and Elaine felt a strong surge of renewed hope for her. Intravenous lines ran fluid into her veins; everything that could possibly be done for her was being done. University Hospital was the best place for her to be.

'Ah, Miss Stewart, I'm glad you're here. I'd like to have a few words with you.' Raoul came over to her before she could leave the room and she felt herself beginning to blush. Then he was shepherding her out as though he had urgent professional matters to discuss with her. With his hand on her upper arm he marched her to the stairwell beside the elevators; the stairs were quite deserted. Once there she pulled away from him and backed up against a wall.

'Are you all right, Elaine?' he said, his voice soft with concern and his expression strained.

'What do you think?' she said defensively as his nearness unnerved her completely.

Things could never be the same between them again, not now that she had experienced such intimacy with him and had abandoned herself totally to the passion that he had so effortlessly aroused in her. From now on every time she looked at him she would remember in full force the delicious feel of him in her arms; would remember the heady power of his pleasure in her. Surely that must count for something, she thought desperately.

She was close to losing her composure. 'You don't have to concern yourself that I'll make any sort of trouble for you...any sort of demands.' She strove to make her voice sound matter-of-fact. 'As far as I'm concerned the incident is closed...and, as you said, it will never happen again.'

There was a frown on his face as he looked at her. 'I'm not worried about that—it's you I'm worried about. Don't be bitter, love. What happened between us was a perfectly natural thing...and it wasn't planned. We both enjoyed it.'

'Ha! If we both enjoyed it so much how come I look so bloody awful and you don't look so hot yourself?' she ground out, wondering with half her mind how she found the courage to talk to him like that when she was weeping inside and when she so longed to be held by him. 'Yes, I have to admit I did enjoy it. It was what you said after that I found insulting.'

'At least we're talking. That's something,' he said cynically.

'And don't talk to me about being bitter,' she went on, unheeding, 'when your whole life is geared to being bitter.' They were talking quietly, yet with a fierce intensity, mindful that they were standing in a public walkway.

His pale face should have warned her but she did not heed it. Relentlessly she lashed out at him, fuelled by her own hurt. 'Raoul. . .what happened to you. . .to your child. . .was tragic. But we see tragedy around us every day. . . We live tragedy.' She faced him with clenched fists. 'We see how people face up to it; we see their tremendous courage. You can't let it destroy your life. One day you have to live again.'

'You speak from personal experience, do you?' he said quietly, dangerously, his eyes glittering with anger.

For the first time she had a sense of how formidable he could be yet she went blundering on, unable to help herself. 'No,' she said, facing up to him, 'but I like to think that empathy is one of my better qualities. Your wife left you. That's an everyday occurrence!' She was goading him, forcing him out. 'It's all right to want somebody. . .'

'Not for me,' he said, staring at her incredulously, his voice hoarse with raw emotion. 'It wasn't an everyday occurrence for me. It only happened once to me and I don't give a damn how common it is. It wasn't common for me.'

'You can't continue your life in a haze of self-pity, making other people suffer for it. How do you think I felt when you said, "We shouldn't have done this" . . . when it was too late? You. . .you dismissed me. You made me feel so. . .used.' There was a catch in her voice now as humiliation burned in her.

'What the hell do you know about anything? If I used you then you used me.' His face was taut with emotion. 'How dare you tell me that what I feel is self-pity? You've scarcely begun to live.'

'I wouldn't be a nurse if I didn't know something

about how people feel,' she said tightly, hastily wiping away the few tears that had squeezed themselves from her eyes.

'I can see that you've studied your psychology pretty thoroughly,' he said with deft sarcasm, apparently ignoring her tears. At any other time she might have laughed.

'I. . .I feel so desperately sorry for what happened to you. . . Raoul, I do understand. . .as far as it's possible for anyone to understand someone else's pain,' she said earnestly, keeping her voice down. 'But I do think that what you are being is a little self-indulgent.'

'What. . .?'

She hurried on, 'And you're using that to keep your distance from anyone who might want to get close to you. That's very convenient, Raoul. You. . .you hurt them. . .and you do it deliberately because you've got the perfect excuse!' She stopped then, breathing heavily. Those words had somehow come to her; had tumbled out as though of their own volition; she had had no premeditated idea that she would say that. Through her pain an odd sense of amazement filled her.

'That's a bitchy thing to say,' he said, speaking through taut lips. 'Let me tell you something about yourself. Just because a man makes love to you do you think he's going to devote the rest of his life to you?'

'No. . .'

'No? That assumption is pretty common in the female sex, from my experience,' he went on relentlessly.

'I've noticed the reverse. . .'

'Jill Parkes is recommending you for the headship,' he interrupted her, 'and you're vacillating. Don't you think that your hesitation is a refusal to say yes to life, as you put it?'

'No. It's. . .not a step one can take lightly. . .'

'Quite!' he said. 'Neither do I take my decisions

lightly. The ones I have made suit me.'

'You said your work is your life,' she went on, feeling now that she might as well say all that was on her mind. . .now that any possibility of love or friendship between them appeared to have been destroyed. 'I bet your wife had reason to feel bitter.'

'Be quiet!' He ground the words out, his eyes blazing. Stepping forward abruptly, he grasped her upper arms tightly and gave her a little shake. 'What do you know? Pull yourself together and be quiet.'

At his touch the fight went out of her and she felt suddenly weak and tremulous. It was with relief that she heard the sound of the nearby elevator come to a halt; heard it disgorge its passengers; heard the sound of their muted conversation. Raoul let go of her and stepped back. Never had she seen him look so haggard—not even when they had been up for twenty-four hours doing a transplant—and her heart went out to him in an agony of frustrated longing.

A nurse came down the stairs and hurried past them, giving Elaine a quick, perceptive glance. Seeing the opportunity to get away, she turned from him.

'Goodnight, Dr Kenton,' she said. 'From now on I shall confine my remarks to professional matters.'

With that she began to walk quickly down the stairs, not looking back. The nurse who had gone ahead of her was, Elaine realised as she caught up with her on the stairs, the one who had been with Mrs Ritter in the intensive care unit.

'Hi,' the nurse greeted her, slowing down so that she could catch up, 'I thought you looked rather fraught up there. Are you OK?'

'Yes. . .' Elaine tried to smile, not very successfully.

'I wouldn't get involved with him if I were you. . . fantastic though he is,' the other nurse said shrewdly.

'He's a workaholic. He'll hurt you the way he hurt his wife.'

'Did you. . .know his wife?' Elaine asked, stopping her flight.

'I sure did. She used to be a biochemist here until after their daughter died. After that she couldn't hack it any more. . . Gave up hospital work, I think.'

'What about him?' Elaine asked, seeing that her colleague was willing to talk. 'I. . .wish I could understand him. . .'

'He worked like a mad thing. Always seemed to be in the hospital, day and night. I thought some of the other guys were bad. . .but him!' the nurse said ruefully. 'How could you stand to be married to someone like that?'

A group of chattering doctors overtook them on the stairs and they went their separate ways. By the time that Elaine was at the ground floor she had regained her outward composure. She hoped fervently that the patient Angie was still waiting for her; she desperately needed that supper and the promised wine.

Then, with a stab of alarm, she realised that if she was to apply for the job of acting head of Unit 2 she would have to get a reference from Dr Raoul Kenton.

CHAPTER NINE

THAT night Elaine slept no better than she had done the night before. As she tossed and turned all anger dissipated, to be replaced by a sad sense of loss. She considered that she had been terribly rude to Raoul. Recalling the words that she had spoken, she shuddered mentally at what she had said—going over the scene again and again. She was not naturally a vindictive person and could not maintain animosity for the sake of it.

At last she achieved a certain peace, having come to the conclusion that she had to apologise if they were to maintain a reasonable working relationship. Life would become impossible if other colleagues noticed any animosity between them. Somehow she would have to find a way of approaching him. Work in the operating room depended very much on an excellent team spirit and complete co-operation.

Such an opportunity came on his next operating day. The operating list was full, involving several long cases. Elaine watched and waited for an opening and found one as Raoul began scrubbing at the sinks for his next case after his assistant surgeons had already gone into the operating room of their unit. Resolutely but inwardly terrified she marched up to him, the rehearsed sentences on the tip of her tongue.

'Dr Kenton,' she said, to get his attention, 'I want to apologise for being so awfully rude to you the other day.'

He paused in his scrub routine, slowly turning his head to observe her flushed face. 'So you want to kiss and make up, do you?' he drawled, after observing her for a long moment as though he was enjoying the spectacle of her squirming. . .like a fish on the end of a hook, she thought. . .and the sight of her deepening flush.

'Please put it down to my emotional state at the time. It's absolutely no business of mine how you conduct your life.' She gabbled the words like an actor saying a set piece.

'Is that so?' he said, not helping her.

'Yes. I hope you'll forgive me. . .so that we can get back to some sort of workable relationship.'

Having said that, she would have turned on her heel and marched back into the operating room quickly had he not reached forward and put a restraining hand, a wet hand, on her upper arm.

'I'm not sure I believe you,' he said slowly, his grip tight.

'Please. . .you must!' she said frantically. This was not the way she had pictured it.

Deliberately he reached forward and pulled down her face mask and then pulled down his own to reveal the set line of his mouth.

'If you really do want to kiss and make up you'd better get on with it. . .while we're still alone. . .then I might believe you.' His eyes were dark with an unfathomable expression as she stared at him aghast.

'But. . . I. . .' she began.

'Get on with it, Miss Stewart,' he urged softly, his mouth quirking in a cynical grin. 'You take the initiative this time. . .then we can forget all about it. Hmm? Then we can concentrate on what we're here for. . .work.'

As he stood perfectly still, waiting, she leaned forward awkwardly and brushed his lips with hers. When she would have withdrawn she found that he moved with her so that the light contact turned into a proper kiss, a heart-rending physical communication. . . for her. Breathlessly she withdrew from him, pulling her arm out of his grasp, her chest heaving with emotion. Like some Victorian damsel in distress, she thought in a moment of frantic weakness.

'We all say things we wished afterwards we hadn't said,' he reminded her. 'I think we're quits now.'

In the days that remained until Christmas, when the hectic routine became even more hectic before eventually tailing off, Elaine avoided all but very necessary professional contact with Raoul Kenton. All that time she was aware that he was watching her. Many times he had attempted to approach her and, at the last minute, she had deflected his attention by joining one of her colleagues or leaving the room if he came in when she was working alone. Maybe he wanted to apologise too, she speculated. . .scared to give him the chance.

She sensed what would happen if they made any tentative moves to assuage their mutual attraction—he would let it go so far and no further and she would suffer. It seemed that he was both avoiding her and moving towards her at the same time, if that were possible, and she suspected that she was really doing the same.

All the time she longed to put back the clock so that perhaps they could do things differently. There was no regret that they had made love; the only regret was that it looked as though it would never happen again.

'Done your Christmas shopping yet?' That was the catch-phrase of the day, while the rueful answer was, 'What do you think?' Gradually a festive spirit began to invade the entire operating suite. The usual plastic Christmas tree that was put up in the entrance foyer of the operating room every year was once again hauled out of its box, set in place and decorated with coloured baubles. A bunch of plastic mistletoe hung near it, reminding Elaine sharply of the Christmas dance.

Carla Ritter had been transferred to an acute care ward and hoped to be allowed to go home for Christmas. When Elaine went to see her on 22 December she was walking around the ward, dressed in a faded robe. Her wispy brown hair had been washed and styled in a becoming way; there was no sign of the jaundice that had been the hallmark of her disease. Beside her bed her ten-year-old daughter sat in a chair looking on proudly, happily, as her mother made the circuit of the small four-bedded ward.

'I'm going to feel better this Christmas than I did for the last one,' Carla said to Elaine, 'and, I can tell you, I'm really going to enjoy this one. When I came round from that operation I felt as though every bone in my body was broken. I feel pretty good now.' Her face had the characteristic rounded appearance from the anti-inflammatory cortisone drugs that she had been taking.

'Got your tree up yet?' Elaine asked Carla's daughter.

'Oh, yes,' the girl said, smiling shyly. 'We've had it up for two weeks—all ready for Mum to come home.'

'I'll be thinking of you,' Elaine smiled back. All things seemed to fall into perspective when she looked at Carla and her family, who had arranged their lives around Carla's illness and had adapted to those circumscribed lives, obviously grateful for every day that she remained with them. That was the power of love. A lesser family might have split up; might have abandoned her to cope alone.

'I'll see you when you come back for your check-ups sometimes, Carla. Have a good holiday. And take care.'

'I sure will!' The frail woman confirmed her intention to make the most of what she had.

*   *   *

'Want to come Christmas shopping with me on the twenty-fourth, Angie?' Elaine asked her friend as they cleared away used linen and instruments at the end of the day. 'As usual I've left a lot of stuff to the last minute.'

'Sure, love to,' Angie agreed readily, picking up used linen and bundling it into a plastic laundry bag. 'Do you want to spill your guts again? Maybe I'll start charging for counselling. I reckon I could make a decent living at it, judging by the rate you're going.'

'I think we're quits, Angie, fifty-fifty. No, I have nothing more to add at the moment,' she sighed. 'Just general angst.'

'Hey, girls!' Matt Ferrera stood in the open doorway looking dishevelled in a crumpled scrub suit, his hair untidy from where he had raked off his operating cap at the end of the operating list. 'Want to come out for a drink later, Elaine? Christmas and all that?' His flirtatious brown eyes were fixed on Elaine as she sorted through the used instruments, her hands covered by rubber gloves.

Just as she was about to say, Sorry, not tonight, Raoul walked into the room and she was certain that he had heard the request. Instinctively she looked at him and their eyes met; his expression was unreadable, his mouth set in a firm line. He too had removed his operating cap, showing his thick, pale hair that she had run her hands through exultantly such a short time ago. Now he seemed remote, untouchable.

'I think I may have left my pen in here,' he said to no one in particular. 'Probably on the anaesthetic machine.'

Angie scrabbled through the disarray on the machine. 'This it, Dr Kenton?' She held up a black and gold pen, the sort that anyone would be sorry to lose.

'That's it. Thanks.' Instead of leaving the room he put

the chart that he was carrying down on the anaesthetic machine and began to write in it there.

Matt stood indecisively in the doorway and cleared his throat suggestively. Not normally reticent, he probably hesitated to pursue his hoped-for love life in front of his boss. 'Er. . .what's the verdict then, Elaine?' he said, shifting his weight from foot to foot.

'All right,' she said, more to bring the conversation to an end than anything else. Sometimes she wished that Matt would not be so persistent when he clearly was not serious about her nor she about him.

'Usual place?' he queried.

'Yes,' she said abruptly. Sure that Raoul had heard his offer, there was no way that she would refuse it in his hearing and let him know indirectly that she was pining for him. Not that she thought it mattered to him; it was more a self-esteem thing, she told herself.

As Matt made his exit, grinning, Angie began to hump heavy laundry bags out of the room so that, alarmingly, Elaine found herself alone in the room with Raoul, wondering how she could justify making a quick exit. Not sure exactly what she was afraid of with him. . .his anger or her own weaknesses. . .she bent her head over her task.

'And where is the ''usual place'', Miss Stewart?' he queried her softly.

'Not the fourteenth floor of the MacKenzie Tower,' she said as quick as a flash. Then she was appalled by what she had said—it had just come out.

There was a flash of something like admiration in his regard and a quickly stifled humour as they looked at each other silently before Angie came bursting back into the room.

'That laundry chute's blocked again!' she moaned, oblivious to any 'atmosphere'. 'Wouldn't you know it? Just when we've got about two hundred bags to put down the thing! You'd think the guys at the bottom end would keep things moving.' With that remark she hauled out the next bag.

Without another word Raoul picked up his papers and left the room, leaving Elaine with a poignant sense of loss. Even though there was tension when she was working with him now, at least she was with him... something that she found she wanted more than anything. Now she would not see him until after Christmas.

Angie came back. 'Was he coming on to you?' she said crudely. 'I get the impression he hasn't finished with you yet.'

'No, he wasn't,' she said. 'Oh, Angie, I'm going to miss him. I know it's stupid. He's going to have his Christmas dinner in a hotel. Imagine that.'

'So what? My mother's greatest ambition is to have Christmas dinner in a hotel. She says so every year.' Angie laughed and Elaine joined in.

It was a relief to be sitting in a dimly lit bar with Matt some time later. The bar, conveniently located in a big international hotel within a short walking distance of the hospital, was a favourite haunt of some of the medical and nursing staff. As they had walked over, enjoying the crisp, cold air after the enclosed atmosphere of the operating room, a few early flakes of snow had fallen about them.

There were few other people there at this time. Elaine chattered to hide the heartache engendered by the knowledge that she was with the wrong man, much as she appreciated Matt's company.

'You're very quiet, Matt,' she commented after a particularly long pause that seemed unusually tense after they had seated themselves in the plush chairs and had been served their drinks.

'I've been wanting to ask you something,' he said, his curly dark head bent over his glass of light beer.

'You know that my residency will be over in a few weeks. I'm thinking of applying for a job in Western Canada with another liver team. If that fails I may apply for something similar in the States.'

'That's great! You're chances of getting it should be pretty good. You're the best senior resident that I've ever worked with,' she said sincerely. 'I'll miss you too.'

'I was wondering if you'd come with me,' he blurted out, his usual confidence in abeyance. 'There are jobs for nurses on the liver team. . .I took the trouble to find out.'

That was the last thing Elaine had been expecting and her stunned expression would have felled a lesser man, she felt sure. Just when she thought that he might be proposing marriage to her he went on quickly, 'We could live together. Then we'd have each other in a strange place.'

'Now. . .I want to be quite sure of this, Matt,' she said slowly, leaning forward. 'Are you proposing marriage to me?'

'Well. . .no. I don't think I'm ready for marriage yet,' he said thoughtfully, 'but I guess we could get married if you really want that.'

'Just like that!' she said incredulously.

Matt had the grace to blush as he grinned sheepishly. 'I know that sounds pretty awful. I didn't mean. . .'

'I'm afraid you did mean, Matt,' she said soberly. 'You don't want to marry me any more than I want to marry you. I think you want me with you because you're used to being part of a large family and you'd feel lonely on your own. Hmm?'

Surprisingly Matt said nothing for a long time so that she leaned forward and put a hand over his. 'I'll just miss you like hell,' she said, 'but the other wouldn't work and you know it.'

'I didn't think you would agree,' he said. 'It was worth a try. Is it Raoul Kenton?'

'What?' Her heart stilled.

'Is there something between you and Raoul Kenton?'

'Why do you think that?' She stalled for time, not wanting to admit it to Matt who was liable to joke about it subtly at the wrong time.

'He's been in a bloody awful mood lately. He sure needs a woman. . .and there are vibes in your direction. He watches you, too, when he thinks no one's noticing,' Matt said, an edge of bitterness in his voice.

'Maybe so; maybe not,' she said, tense herself now. 'If he wants me he has a very peculiar way of showing it. No. . .I don't think I'm in the running.'

'You would like to be?'

'Frankly, yes.' There was no point in lying to Matt to protect his ego; he was too intelligent for that.

'You're in love with him, aren't you? I can see that for myself now.'

'I don't know. . .'

'Well, he's a lucky guy. I don't suppose he knows it, otherwise he would be taking action.'

'He's oblivious, Matt,' she said, her voice catching. That Raoul had accepted her for sexual release was another matter. . .and she was not about to recount *that* incident to Matt.

'Stupid, more like it,' he said scathingly. 'As much as I admire the guy he seems to be thick when it comes to women. I know he had a pretty awful time when his kid was sick and then died but that was quite a while ago.'

'Yes. . .' she said softly, 'but who are we to talk, really? I'm coming to see that. We haven't been through it.'

'He needs something, or someone, to give him a push.

What he sees in Della I've no idea. She's an ice-maiden if ever there was one.'

'Are they lovers, do you think?' she asked tentatively, fearing the answer, staring down into her glass of white wine as she absently twirled the stem.

'Doubt it,' he said. 'I have a feeling that it's convenient for him to have people think so.'

'Why?'

'I'm not sure. I think he would want someone softer, more thoughtful, more introspective. Someone like you.'

'Oh, don't tease, Matt!' She attempted to make light of it. 'Drink up. The next one's on me.'

'OK, same again.' Matt looked around him. 'This place is dead. Maybe the rest of the population knows something that we don't know—like an impending snow storm or something. Anyway, kid, if you change your mind about coming with me just let me know. You've got weeks yet.'

'Thanks for the thought, Matt,' she said. 'After this drink I have to get home to feed my cat.'

CHAPTER TEN

'Go AND call your dad, Elaine, and tell him dinner will be ready in precisely fifteen minutes. He's having a nap, I believe. It'll take him that long to get himself up.' Mrs Stewart, her face flushed from peering into a hot oven, straightened up and looked at her daughter. 'Then would you mind giving Joanne a call over at the Stevensons' place, dear? She said she'd be gone half an hour. . .and now look at the time. . .it's more like two hours! She gets back from Texas, not having seen us for six months, and she's over at the Stevensons' place most of the time! I think she still has a crush on that Jamie Stevenson.'

'Maybe. She always was one to get out of the chores,' Elaine said mildly, surveying the organised chaos in the large, warm kitchen of her parents' house—the place that had been her childhood home. 'Just relax, Mum. I'll round her up, and Dad too, then I'll help you serve.'

'Thanks, dear. I'm just going to finish off the gravy and then everything's ready,' Mrs Stewart said, resuming her task of stirring gravy in a cooking pot on the top of the stove. 'I've got everything else wrapped in foil in the oven to keep it hot. Every year at this point I think that we should have gone to a hotel. Maybe we will next year, much as I love Christmas at home.'

'You never admitted that before,' Elaine smiled, while a sharp stab of remembrance hit her at the mention of a hotel.

'It's an admission that I'm getting old,' her mother commented.

Raoul was not far from Elaine's thoughts, even though she had resolutely tried to push all thoughts of him aside as she and her family had prepared the usual dinner which they always ate at about two o'clock in the afternoon on Christmas Day. Now those thoughts came back in full force as she checked her wrist-watch to see that the time was half-past one. Perhaps by now he would be sitting in a hotel somewhere. . .

'Are you day-dreaming?' her mother asked perceptively. 'Better call Dad.'

'I'm going right now,' she said, coming back to reality.

As she slowly mounted the main staircase of the rambling three-storey house towards her father's study on the top floor she thought of how she and Raoul had lain together on his bed in the MacKenzie Tower; how he had kissed her hungrily and she had responded. Now it seemed like a million years away and she pined for him.

'Dad. . . Dad?' she called as she arrived on the top floor landing. 'Dinner's going to be ready in precisely fifteen minutes.'

The response that she had expected did not come. Instead there was a muted sound that was very much like a moan of pain.

'Dad?' she said tentatively as she went through the door of his study off the third-floor landing.

The large desk that stood in the centre of the room was sideways to the door. As she entered she saw her father sitting in the chair at the desk, slumped forward with both his arms wrapped round the centre of his body as though in intense pain. His face was contorted and his breath coming in gasps, as though he was trying to prevent himself from crying out.

'Oh, no. . .' The involuntary cry escaped from her as she rushed forward. In a second she was kneeling on the carpet beside his chair. 'Dad, what's wrong?'

'Terrible. . .pain. . .' He managed to get the words

out through gritted teeth. Elaine could see that his face was covered with perspiration, the skin an unhealthy yellowish-grey colour.

'Where, Dad?' she said urgently, taking his hand in hers. 'Where's the pain?'

'My chest,' he gasped out, 'and all around here. . .' He made a motion with his hands, indicating the area of his diaphragm. 'Oh. . .my God. . .the pain. . .I can hardly bear it.'

'Dad, come and lie down on the sofa,' she urged him, standing up and grasping his arm.

'No. . .I tried that,' he protested. 'The pain feels worse when I lie down.'

Feeling sick herself—with worry—Elaine tried to collect her thoughts. 'Dad, have you got pain in your neck or your jaw? Or does it radiate down your left arm?'

'No,' he groaned out the word. 'It's just across here. . .and in my lower chest. Do you think I'm having a heart attack?'

That fear had been in her mind from the moment she had seen his pale, contorted face. Now other possibilities were passing like lightning through her brain. He did not appear to be bleeding. . .at least not rapidly, otherwise he would have collapsed by now, she decided frantically, her fingers searching for his pulse. 'Do you feel nauseated?'

'Yes, I do,' he confirmed.

'I want to feel your pulse, Dad,' she said, trying to sound calm. 'Then I want to get my bag with the stethoscope in it. . .I want to listen to your chest and take your blood pressure. It. . .it may not necessarily be your heart.' The majority of people, she knew, were terrified of the possibility of a myocardial infarction. . . a heart attack. Although the awful fear was uppermost in her consideration, other possibilities were there too.

What a thing to happen on Christmas Day! She wanted to keep the knowledge as long as possible from her mother—until she had made a tentative diagnosis and decided what to do—although at any minute now her mother would find out what was going on.

Outwardly calm, she placed cool fingers on her father's wrist to feel his radial pulse. That pulse rate was rapid, tachycardia. . .yet the pace was regular and steady. Elaine frowned.

'I'm going to run down and get my bag from the second floor, Dad,' she said, knowing that her own voice sounded high with anxiety.

'What's going on up there?' Her mother's voice floated up the stairs.

Elaine ran down the next flight of the stairs to grab her nursing bag from her bedroom, in which she kept equipment for basic resuscitation and medical assessment, before answering her mother.

'Dad's not feeling well,' she called down, before racing back up to the top floor.

As she helped her father to take off his shirt she heard her mother following her up. First she listened to his chest with her stethoscope, her own heart pounding in fear as she listened for the tell-tale signs that would indicate that a blood clot was lodged in his coronary artery. The heartbeat would sound abnormal—not the usual two-beat rhythm, the 'lup dup' sound, that could be heard on auscultation from the normal healthy heart.

Frowning in concentration as she listened she felt some of the terrible fear subside. To her, the heart sounded abnormally fast but otherwise normal. Quickly she put a thermometer in his mouth and then wrapped the cuff of a sphygmomanometer around his upper arm to take his blood pressure.

'What on earth's going on?' Her mother burst into the room, breathless from having climbed the stairs. Her husband—with the thermometer in his mouth—could not answer her, while Elaine had her ears plugged with the stethoscope as she took her father's blood pressure so Mrs Stewart had to hover uncertainly, waiting.

'He has a bad pain,' Elaine said at last. 'Don't worry, I don't think it's a heart attack.' She addressed both of them as they turned shocked and anxious eyes on her, waiting for reassurance.

'Did you eat breakfast, Dad?' she asked. 'And have you had any alcohol to drink?'

'He didn't have any breakfast, I can tell you that,' her mother said quickly. 'What do you think it is, Elaine?'

'I had a glass of beer,' Mr Stewart gasped, not able to keep the fear from his voice as he sat with his eyes closed, leaning forward with his arms wrapped around his middle. Just then he looked exactly what he was: a tired, over-worked, middle-aged man who did not get enough relaxation. Elaine felt as though her heart were bleeding for him as she longed to take him in her arms and to ease his pain.

'I think it could be acute pancreatitis. That is, inflammation of the pancreas. It sometimes comes on after drinking alcohol, especially when there hasn't been any food intake,' Elaine explained. How much alcohol her father habitually drank, she had no idea. She didn't think it was much but she just didn't know for sure. 'I'm afraid you'll have to go to hospital, Dad, to get it checked out. I. . .I'm pretty sure it's not your heart. The symptoms aren't quite right for that.'

'Why on earth isn't Joanne back?' her mother fretted, her usually calm face pinched with worry. 'This would have to happen while she's out.'

'It's all right, Mum,' Elaine said, putting her equipment back in her bag, sensitive to her mother's tacit dismissal of her because Joanne was available. 'We don't need Joanne right now. Look, we'll call Dr Jensen and have him meet us at the emergency department at University Hospital. He is still your GP, isn't he?'

'Yes, but. . .oh, my God. . .it's that awful Dr Rankin,' her mother said suddenly, putting her hand up to her mouth in consternation. 'Dr Jensen's on vacation over Christmas and the other guy's doing a locum for him. I can't stand him, Elaine. We can't get him! He's arrogant. . .I just don't like him.' Mrs Stewart was adamant. 'There must be some other way. . .'

'I expect he's a good doctor, Mum,' Elaine protested, aware of the precious minutes ticking by.

'Not him. . .please!' her mother pleaded.

Elaine came to a quick decision. 'We can't waste any more time, Mum.' Then she turned to her father. 'I'm going to call one of the doctors I know at the hospital and get someone to see you, Dad, in the emergency department. You run next door, Mum. Ask if you can use their phone while I use ours. Call Joanne first and ask her to get back here right away. I want her to go with him in the ambulance.'

'The ambulance. . .?' her mother whispered, her face appearing to crumple as tears formed in her frightened eyes.

'Yes. After you've spoken to Joanne dial the emergency number for an ambulance and tell them to get here as soon as possible.'

She gave her mother a hug, her own emotion vying with her need to organise and to stay calm. Mrs Stewart, who was normally calmness itself and had always been so when her children were ill, seemed to be in a state of shock as she looked at the ashen face of her husband and heard his gasps of pain.

'Can you do that?' Elaine queried, gently but firmly. 'Remember, Joanne first. . .make it fast. . .then the emergency number.'

'Yes. . .'

'Go now, Mum. He's going to be all right.'

'Will. . .will Dad be all right while we're both on the phone?' Mrs Stewart's voice shook as she asked the question.

'He'll be fine.'

As her mother clattered down the stairs Elaine turned to her father. 'Lean forward on the desk, Dad, and put your head down. Everything's going to be all right. I'm going to leave you for a few minutes to make some phone calls.'

Downstairs in her own room she lifted up the extension telephone. She hesitated for only a moment, overcoming her reluctance, before she punched in the familiar number of the locating service at University Hospital. A firm decision formed itself in her consciousness, spurred on by the mental image of her father's contorted face. Whatever he had wrong with him it was something serious. . .

'Locating,' a voice answered promptly.

'I have to contact Dr Raoul Kenton urgently,' she said, her voice quivering. 'This is Elaine Stewart, RN, from the operating room. Do you have a number for him? Or a pager number? I think he was going to be eating his Christmas dinner in a hotel. . .I don't know which one.'

'Hold the line, please.'

Elaine found that she didn't care if they thought she was in the operating room now and was calling from there, perhaps with an operation in the offing; all she wanted to do was to speak to Raoul Kenton. Above all, she trusted him. Whether he would welcome her call was another matter; she would have to risk it. . .

'I have his home number,' the efficient voice informed her. 'I'm going to try there first, but if he's not there I'll try the pager.'

'Thank you.'

The line went dead as she was put on hold. Then, in a matter of seconds, surprisingly, she heard his voice—that familiar deep sound that had a calming effect—cutting through her anxiety. 'Raoul Kenton here.'

'Hi. . .it's Elaine Stewart. . .the OR nurse,' she said, in case he should have a momentary loss of memory regarding her identity. 'I'm very sorry to call you on Christmas Day. I'm calling from my parents' home. My father's very ill. . .I think he has acute pancreatitis. . .at least, that's my diagnosis.'

'When did this happen, Elaine?' his calm voice cut in, a sound that forced her to bite her lip hard for a few seconds as tears started in her eyes.

'Just a few moments ago,' she said. 'I was wondering if you could please recommend someone who could see him in the emergency department—someone who knows something about that disease. Our usual GP's on vacation. . .and I. . .I don't want my father to just turn up there and have to see an intern. We've called an ambulance.'

'What makes you think it's acute pancreatitis, Elaine?'

His steady voice cut through her anxiety and she could have wept with relief as she rapidly described her father's symptoms, not caring now that her voice trembled.

'He has a low blood pressure, a bit of a fever and, although he has some tachycardia, the heart sounds normal to me when I listen to his chest. And. . .and the type and location of the pain isn't quite right for a myocardial infarct. . .I think,' she spoke rapidly. 'The pain's excruciating. It's mainly epigastric pain, radiating up into the chest but not the jaw, neck or left arm. He's nauseated, too.'

'How far are you from the hospital?'

'It's about a twenty-minute ride by car.'

'And the ambulance is on its way?' Not once had he indicated that he was less than pleased with her call.

'Yes. . .'

'I'll meet you in the emergency department. I should be there in about twenty minutes myself.'

'I. . .I didn't mean for you to come yourself,' she said. 'I didn't want to—'

'I'll be there,' he cut in. 'I'll get Dr Jerome Lyle to come in to see your father. He's the pancreas expert and I happen to know that he's in town today.'

'Th-thank you.' Her voice broke. 'I. . .we're so worried.'

'Take it easy, sweetheart,' he said. 'Just get your-selves there as fast as you can. I'll take care of the rest.'

She almost wished he wouldn't call her 'sweetheart'; it made her think that he cared for her.

'What is it, Raoul?' A voice that Elaine recognised as belonging to Della Couts sounded clearly in the back-ground. Obviously he was spending at least part of Christmas Day with Dr Couts in his own house.

If she had not been so anxious about her father the sense of sickening denouement that she felt might have made her hang up then and tell him not to bother—that she would find someone else. As it was she did no such thing.

CHAPTER ELEVEN

AFTERWARDS Elaine could scarcely remember how she had got to the hospital, so automatic had been her response, sick with apprehension as she drove the familiar route in Joanne's car.

It had all been something of a nightmare. Joanne and her mother had gone in the ambulance with her father and she had driven behind so that they would have one car at the hospital. To complicate matters there had been a light fall of snow, making the roads slightly slippery.

The ambulance had arrived promptly at the house and Joanne had persuaded the ambulance attendants to give Mr Stewart a strong painkiller, having agreed with Elaine that he most likely had acute pancreatitis. When Elaine had finally walked into the emergency department of University Hospital the others had already been there for some minutes and had already seen Raoul Kenton briefly, who had managed in short order to round up Dr Jerome Lyle.

'I'm very grateful to you.' Elaine walked up to Raoul, seeing him standing momentarily alone in the wide main corridor of the department outside the examination room where her father was, presumably, being seen. His dynamic presence made everything seem much more hopeful. He stood with hands in pockets, waiting.

'Hi,' he greeted her, turning towards her with his astute eyes probing her face to assess her mood. 'Your father's in there with your mother and sister. Everything's fine so far.'

At his gentleness tears pricked her eyes. She was beginning to feel warm at last, in her winter boots and heavy coat, whereas before she had been shivering from delayed shock. Shrugging out of the coat, she stood with him. 'Thank you very, very much for what you've done; for speaking to Dr Lyle. I hope this hasn't spoiled your day beyond recall. . .or his.' Obliquely she was referring to the fact that he had been with Dr Couts.

He looked at her consideringly, a slight smile on his mouth. In the blue jeans and casual dark blue sweater that he wore over a plaid shirt he looked very relaxed, very male. 'Perhaps I should thank you,' he said, 'for helping me get through the day. There's always the feeling that you *ought* to be enjoying yourself, which somehow brings a certain pressure to bear which assures that you *won't* enjoy yourself.' From the way he said it she could not be sure whether he was being facetious.

'Hmm. . .' she said, thinking of the lovingly prepared dinner that was awaiting her family at her parents' home and that had so hastily been abandoned for the mad dash to the hospital. 'I can't say that I needed anything to help me get through the day—certainly not this.'

Oddly she had wanted to see him. Now her wish had been granted but at a strange price. Fate worked in mysterious ways. 'It. . .it's pretty busy here for Christmas Day,' she added, looking around them and blinking rapidly to disperse the tears.

'A lot of lonely people about,' he murmured, standing casually with his hands still in the pockets of his jeans. 'They come in here for a bit of human contact. . .even if it means attempting suicide first.'

They stood back against a wall to allow a stretcher with an accident patient on it to be pushed by them and Elaine looked briefly at the wan face on the pillow.

'We have to be grateful for what we have,' she said quietly. 'I. . .I hope your Christmas was not too lonely.' Again she thought of the photograph of the pale, smiling child beside his bed in the on-call room and felt intuitively that he was also thinking of her, as he must have done every Christmas.

'Not as bad as some,' he murmured meaningfully as he stood close to her as though protecting her.

That was an admission of sorts, she thought distractedly. At any other time she might have seen it as a hopeful opening to communication between them. As it was she was having difficulty controlling her features when she so wanted to turn her face into his broad chest and howl like a baby and to feel his arms firmly round her.

'I'm pretty sure your father's going to be fine,' he said gently, interpreting her fraught expression without making her feel embarrassed that he had done so. Momentarily he put a hand on her shoulder. 'You were quite right, I think, about it being pancreatitis. Your knowing that must have helped to reassure both your parents.' Then he slid his arm around her comfortingly, giving her a quick squeeze. 'Hang in there, kid! You're doing great.'

Elaine looked at the floor, fighting back the tears that she had managed to keep in tight check before when she had had to take charge. 'Thank you,' she said softly. 'I. . .hope I am right. My father was terrified, of course, that it was his heart. Anyway, thank you for. . .'

Just then Joanne came out of the room and walked briskly over to them. In the six months since Elaine had last seen her sister Joanne seemed to have become more attractive than ever. She had, it seemed, lost weight so that her figure looked gorgeous in the simple, chic black skirt and matching cashmere sweater that she wore. Her hair, naturally the same light bronzy brown as Elaine's, had been streaked with blonde highlights and was now brushed back from her face and held at the nape of her neck with a black silk bow.

'I didn't have a chance to thank you earlier, Dr Kenton,' she said, her voice light and musical as she came towards them with her hand outstretched, her long, slender fingers with the red-painted nails reaching for Raoul's hand. Even in her anxiety she managed to remain sophisticated and charming. Her full red lips were stretched in a smile, showing her beautiful teeth, and her large green eyes held a genuine warmth that the majority of women in her position would not have been able to muster at a time like that.

A light of admiration appeared in Raoul's eyes as he took Joanne's hand. 'As I was telling your sister,' he drawled, looking into Joanne's eyes, 'this has helped me get through the day. I don't enjoy Christmas much at the best of times.'

'I won't ask why,' Joanne said, letting her unconsciously bold eyes rove over his face. 'Suffice it to say that we're enormously grateful and. . .if I can say this without sounding patronising. . . I'd forgotten how good and efficient University Hospital can be.'

'Yes, it is,' Raoul drawled back. 'Better than anything you could find in Texas, I think. And you can live here without having to tote a gun for your own protection, too.'

Joanne made a wry face. 'You're right there,' she said.

'How's Dad?' Elaine interjected, her voice wobbly.

'Pretty good, actually,' Joanne said calmly. 'Dr Lyle's ordered a CT scan. . .he's been getting in touch with the on-call radiologist. Dad has no pain now. They're giving him IV fluids and IV analgesics. He's got a nasogastric tube down now to clear his stomach contents—they've got that hooked up to a suction pump. He won't be able to take anything by mouth for a while. The pancreas needs complete rest. So much for Christmas dinner.'

'What a relief,' Elaine sighed. 'What's the next move?'

'He'll be taken straight to the X-ray department and then he's going to be admitted to the acute care unit for a few days, so Dr Lyle said,' Joanne stated matter-of-factly. She always had been good at hiding her feelings, Elaine remembered as she looked at her sister, feeling pride at her cool competence.

'Can I see him?' she asked.

'I expect so,' Joanne said. 'Then why don't you go on home, Elaine, love? Mum refuses to budge until he's ensconced in Acute Care. Someone ought to go back and make sure everything's OK in the kitchen. . .and people may start dropping by without phoning first. I'll stay here and make sure everything's OK. There's no sense in all of us staying here. Dad's so sedated he doesn't know who's here and who isn't.'

'What about your car? You'll need that to get home,' Elaine said, aware that Raoul was watching this interplay between them with detached interest.

'Get a taxi.'

'I'll drive her home,' Raoul said, addressing Joanne. 'My day is free.'

'You don't have to—' Elaine began.

'It will be a pleasure,' he said.

Like heck! Elaine thought, watching him smile charmingly at her beautiful sister as though he wanted to impress her.

'Excuse me,' Raoul said, 'I'd just like a word or two with Jerome before we depart.'

'He's quite something!' Joanne remarked coolly, turning to look at the back of Dr Kenton as he went into the room to see Dr Lyle. 'What does he do here?'

'He's a surgeon. He does liver transplants, among other things.'

'And you work with him?' Joanne looked at her appraisingly, her interest clearly aroused.

'Mmm, in the operating room,' Elaine said. 'Yes, he is rather nice. . .'

'I should say so! There's no one quite like him where I am and I sure work with a lot of guys,' Joanne murmured admiringly.

'If you can get his interest, good luck,' Elaine commented wistfully. 'He's divorced and had a child that died. I don't think he's much interested in women now.'

'Pity,' Joanne said thoughtfully. 'He certainly inspires me with confidence. I feel a lot better about Dad now. And Dr Lyle seems great, too.'

'Yes. . .well. . .I think we're just trying to distract ourselves.' She took a deep, steadying breath. 'I'm going to see Dad and say goodbye. Then I'll follow your suggestion. . .go home and then come back to see him this evening.'

'Your sister's a lot like you,' Raoul commented later when they were part way back to the Stewart house in his luxury car.

Snow had fallen, covering the road, during their time in the emergency department; it fell around them now— large, gently falling flakes, making them part of a white fairyland. The efficient sweep of the windshield wipers cut a swathe through it as it settled on the glass.

Acutely aware of him in the enclosed space that felt even more enclosed because of the snow on the windows Elaine was perversely glad of the sombre distraction of her father's illness to temper her attraction and her mental turmoil where he was concerned.

With her coat pulled cosily around her, she reclined back in the soft leather seat. 'I always thought we were rather different,' she murmured, glancing quickly at his strong profile, 'my sister and I.'

'She probably doesn't play down her competence the way you tend to do. Apart from that it's easy to tell you're sisters. . .although I think I prefer your haunted, elfin look.'

'Haunted? Yes. . .perhaps I am. . .' she said softly, surprised and touched by the muted compliment. Haunted by you, the thought came to her; haunted by the waste of your life and by my own longing.

'I got the impression that you've been somewhat dominated by your sister,' he said neutrally. 'Would that be right?'

'When we were younger that was true, yes,' she agreed. 'Very perceptive of you from such a brief meeting.'

'You've outgrown it?'

'I think so.'

'By the way,' he said, 'I was asked by the nursing co-ordinator to provide a reference for you. . .about the headship of Unit 2.' He glanced at her briefly.

'I thought you might be asked. I. . .I haven't finally made up my mind about it so I'm asking to be acting head for three months.'

'Hmm. . .' he murmured, enigmatically.

'I can get Dr Richardson to write me a reference if you would rather not,' she said, her voice tight, trying not to sound defensive. Perhaps he was thinking that she was 'fence sitting'. . .

'What makes you think I wouldn't want to write you a reference?' he said.

'What happened between us on the night of the dance,' she said soberly, deciding that there was no point in beating about the bush, 'may have. . .influenced your judgement. . .perhaps against me.'

Traffic lights up ahead turned red and Raoul concentrated on easing the car to a gentle halt on the slippery road. There was very little other traffic. He then took the opportunity to turn his full attention on her. 'Why not *for* you?' he said, his mouth quirked in a slight smile. 'Hmm?'

Elaine felt her face turning red and the breath seemed to stop in her throat. Moistening her dry lips with the tip of her tongue, she strove for composure. 'For me. . . or against me,' she said, skirting the question, 'I want you to know that you don't have to do it if you would rather not.'

'I'll do it,' he said, 'since I work with you probably more than any other doctor. And I can separate my private life from my professional life.'

'Can you?' she said, unable to keep a slight bitterness out of her voice. 'Do you have a private life, Raoul?' Where she found the courage to say that she didn't know. Somehow the shock of her father's illness had suddenly opened her eyes to certain other aspects of reality. 'I had the impression that you did nothing much other than work. You. . .you were rather like a man dying of thirst on that night, even though you have Dr Couts. And, talking of her, I know she was at your place when I called earlier. I hope I didn't break up anything. I'm sorry if I did. . .'

There was a heavy silence in the car, during which Elaine dared not look at him. Her heartbeats were deep and fast to match her breathing. There was an advantage to having a captive audience, she decided; he couldn't get up and walk out. All her life she had wanted things brought out into the open; had not felt comfortable with festering emotion that had a way of destroying one's inner peace.

'There's no point in pretending that what happened between us did not happen,' she said at long last as they pulled to a halt at another set of traffic lights. 'Or that it didn't mean anything. . .at least, to me.' There was a catch in her voice and she gazed bleakly ahead out of the window at the snow that was falling steadily now.

'Maybe you can be impartial. . .I'm not sure that I can be.'

'Dr Couts came to my house to drop something off— the results of some research that she's been doing— before leaving town,' he said coolly.

She had the feeling that in other circumstances, if they had not just left her sick father at the hospital, he would have erupted in anger; there was a definite atmosphere in the car now.

'Anyway,' she persisted, 'thank you in advance for the reference. I definitely do want the job of acting head to help me make up my mind about the permanent job. I. . .I hesitate to get into a situation where I have no time for anything other than work. I've seen what that can do to people. . .and I'm not impressed.'

Again there was a loaded silence as Raoul concentrated on driving, his gloved hands tight on the steering-wheel.

'What are your hopes for the future, long term?' he asked. That question had been asked before, she remembered.

'A head nurse job would be fine for a few years. . . very good experience,' she said quietly. 'It's not easy to see much beyond the next two years. Maybe in the future I would like to teach. I don't want to be one of those teachers who knows a lot of theory but hasn't had much practical experience. . .there are lots of them about. Curiously, they seem to be the most bossy types.'

'I've noticed that myself,' he said, smiling slightly. 'So you're going to be a career woman?'

'I don't really know what that means,' she said carefully. 'If it means foregoing husband and children—a normal family life—then no, definitely not. But I do want to use the training and experience that I've had so far. It would be such a waste otherwise. When I have children I want to be with them.'

'Yes, I agree with you there. Otherwise, what's the point?' he mused.

Thinking that he had not, apparently, extended that philosophy to his wife, Elaine nonetheless bit her tongue.

'Grief is the price we pay for love,' he murmured, apropos of nothing in particular that she had said. The humming of the car engine almost drowned out his voice so she was not sure that she had heard him. Then, as they stopped again at some lights, he turned to her. 'Is it really better to have loved and lost than never to have loved at all, as the poet said? What do you think?'

'Oh, yes. Otherwise it would just be like sleepwalking through life—passing time.'

'You sound very sure,' he said.

'Oh, I'm not really,' she admitted. 'I. . .I can't say that I speak from experience.'

As they neared the Stewart home she suddenly thought about his hotel reservation. 'What about your hotel dinner?' she asked. 'I just remembered about that. I sure hope you haven't missed it.'

'I cancelled it,' he said abruptly.

Elaine sat up straight and leaned towards him. 'Oh, no. . .I'm awfully sorry! It's my fault, isn't it? I probably called you when you were about to go there?'

When he made no comment she went on, 'You must let me make it up to you in some way. . .' The superb dinner that her mother had cooked was still in the oven at their house, wrapped in foil, the table already laid with the silverware, the wine glasses, the flowers in vases, the candelabra. . . They had planned to invite friends over in the evening too, all very casual.

Raoul cut into her thoughts, his tone sardonic, 'I can think of several ways you could make it up to me,' he drawled, 'but I would rather not behave like a man ''dying of thirst in a desert'', or whatever it was you said.'

Was he laughing at her? she thought frantically as her face flamed at the implication of his words. Choosing not to comment, she decided simply to invite him to dinner. 'Would you like to have your Christmas dinner at our place? It's all ready. My mother would never forgive me if I'd let you go away without any food. . .after all you've done for us. . .your kindness. Please stay.'

He turned to look at her then, the pupils of his tawny eyes dark. She read the overt desire in them and her throat constricted with emotion. She knew that he would not touch her, not now when her father lay ill in the place where they both worked. . .if ever. Yet she wanted nothing more than to be held by him. Since they had made love he had kept his distance from her as he had vowed to do. She was confused herself, wanting him yet wanting him to make the first move.

'Since you put it like that. . .so charmingly. . .yes, I will stay. Thank you.'

Elaine relaxed back in the seat and closed her eyes, feeling exhausted. They said no more until they were near the house and then she gave him directions to the quiet, residential street that was bordered by tall trees. The house was set back from the road, with a short semicircular driveway in front of it. Now everything was clothed in white.

'I'm glad you're with me,' she admitted as she unlocked the front door of the house. 'It would seem horribly lonely coming back to an empty house on Christmas Day.'

'I'm glad I'm here, Elaine,' he said simply.

A furry object hurtled past them as she opened the door. 'Cornelius! Damn!' she said, turning abruptly. 'It's my cat. I bring him with me when I'm staying here overnight. He can't wait to get out of the house.' Then they both laughed spontaneously as the cat, having encountered the unexpected snow, came to an abrupt halt and then turned round and hurtled back into the house—all in a few seconds.

'He's a real ice-breaker,' Raoul commented.

The laughter broke some of the tension between them. 'Please take your coat off,' she said when they were inside. 'Come into the sitting-room. Help yourself to some sherry, or whatever.'

Taking off her own coat, she flung it over the bannister of the curving staircase and then put his coat over hers. 'I would like to call the hospital to find out if everything's all right before I serve the dinner.'

'Would you like me to do that?' he asked gently. 'Call the hospital, I mean.'

'Would you?' That was just what she would like, not trusting herself to remain calm while she asked the necessary questions.

'I'm sure your father's fine,' he said.

CHAPTER TWELVE

CHRISTMAS seemed a long way off by the end of January, forgotten for another year now that winter had well and truly arrived for the duration. Heavy snow lay over Gresham, with more promised by the bleak grey hue of the sky over the city.

Life had changed dramatically for Elaine in the past week because Jill Parkes had left and she had become acting head nurse. Not having seen the reference that Raoul Kenton had written for her, she could only assume that it had been good.

Whenever she saw him, which was often, her senses were assailed by the bitter-sweet memory of the Christmas dinner they had shared together before the rest of her family had arrived home. Since then he had been polite, congratulating her on her promotion, yet somehow remote.

'How's your dad these days, Elaine?' Angie Clark asked her on the last Friday of the month as they prepared one of the operating rooms in Unit 2 for the day's operating list early in the morning.

Elaine found that she was having to spread herself rather thinly these days between the four operating rooms that made up her particular unit, with less time to chat, to pass the time of day and to joke with her colleagues.

'Not back at work yet but otherwise OK, thank God,' Elaine said. 'That was a really awful time, I can tell you.' Her father was an editor with a local newspaper, a job that was quite stressful, so she was glad that he was still off.

'Well, Elaine, you've been head nurse for precisely four days,' Cathy chipped in as she busily opened sterile packs for their first case of the day. 'Rather you than me. What does it feel like?'

'As though I'm having to split myself into several pieces,' she laughed ruefully. 'Trying to be in half a dozen places at once. I guess I'll get used to it. . .maybe by the end of the three months! I'll be OK so long as I'm not expected to be all things to all people.'

'Now you know what Jill had to put up with,' Angie said.

'Yeah, that's why she's marrying Joe,' Cathy said, and they all laughed.

'So true!' Elaine grinned.

'Well, all you have to do is to get Matt to take you away from all this,' Angie said as she arranged intubating equipment on the anaesthetic machine.

'I don't need any man to take me away. If I want to go I'll just go, don't worry.'

'If I were you I'd opt for Raoul Kenton,' Cathy said, giving her a broad wink. 'We've all seen the way he devours you with his eyes. I bet he couldn't wait to get his hands on you if you gave him half a chance.'

'Shut up, Cath,' she grinned, her face suffusing with a tell-tale flush. 'I've seen the way you look at Claude.'

'Yeah. . .' Cathy said, with longing. 'If only he would devour me in a like manner. . .'

The surgeons, four of them, were congregated near the scrub sinks outside the room when she emerged. Immediately her eyes went to Raoul Kenton and then quickly away again as he turned to acknowledge her presence, his eyes covertly appraising her. Also there was Dr Pearce Samuels, Mike Richardson and Alex White, a general surgeon. As Elaine hurried to the next room to see how the nurses there were coping with the setting up of the room for the first case she was aware of Raoul watching her progress.

'The telephone's for you,' one of the nurses addressed her, holding out the receiver of the wall-telephone to her.

'Thanks,' she said. In truth she was missing Jill Parkes more than she would care to admit to anyone at that moment, even as she was stimulated mentally by the challenge of being in charge. Maybe, she reflected, it would take her about three weeks to get used to the idea that she was the last line of defence, so to speak.

'Miss Stewart?' The voice on the other end of the line was that of Anne Temple, the operating room co-ordinator. 'I'm afraid that we have a code purple on our hands. I just got word from the chief of surgery, Jerry Claiborne.'

'A code purple,' Elaine repeated the words while her mind was reacting like lightning. That was the disaster code. 'Where? I hope it isn't the airport.' She was holding her breath, her chest tight, waiting for the verdict.

'No, thank God. But it's pretty bad. Four buses and a truck, plus an unspecified number of cars. . .a pile-up, apparently. . .on the South West Highway out of town. Terrible weather conditions. A blizzard.' Her voice was calm. 'What it means for us is that all routine surgery is cancelled in the general surgery units, plus the chest and neurosurgical units, until further notice. We are one of five hospitals that will be taking the injured.'

'I see. . .' Elaine interjected, feeling numb. They all knew the routine in theory; this was the first time that she, or anyone she knew personally, had ever had to put it into practice.

'What you have to do,' the co-ordinator went on, 'is to inform the surgeons and nurses in your unit that the operating list is suspended. There will be a general announcement over the intercom in a few minutes, with further instructions for the surgeons. Leave your rooms free for whatever cases might come in. Keep your telephone lines free. Any cases that you have already prepared, any general abdominal cases, keep the set-up sterile in readiness. Have one nurse in each room scrub and prepare for what comes. Have a major abdominal set-up ready in each room. Any questions?'

'How will we know the order of priority?' she said.

'Each surgeon in your unit will be given a case. Dr Claiborne will decide. You'll be informed by telephone,' Anne Temple said. 'Tell the surgeons first. Then prepare all your rooms. OK?'

'Yes,' Elaine said, her voice betraying her nerves. As she hung up the receiver she experienced a few seconds of something like paralysis before she took a deep breath and turned to the nurses in the room who had paused in their tasks, having got the gist of the conversation. They all looked at each other with wide, scared eyes.

'Code purple,' she stated flatly. 'Hold everything. . . just prepare for a major abdominal. Get scrubbed right away. There's been a pile-up on the South West Highway. All routine stuff suspended. That's all I know at the moment.'

'Oh, hell!' one of the nurses exclaimed, with something like awe in her voice. 'What an awful thing to happen. That's all we need! Imagine trying to rescue people in this weather! And I was hoping for a nice quiet day of hernias and gall bladders and maybe a cyst or two.'

Elaine shrugged wryly. 'Sorry! I'll be back later when I have more news.' With that parting shot she was out of the door, leaving a babble of voices behind her as she hurried towards the surgeons who were still lounging nonchalantly against the scrub sinks. Matt Ferrera and Tony Asher, with the other surgical interns, had joined them and were preparing to scrub for the first case of the day.

'Excuse me, all of you,' she announced nervously to the assembled group, 'I'm afraid there's a code purple...a major road-traffic accident. The operating lists are suspended in our unit. An announcement is going to be made any minute.'

Dr Samuels looked rather as though he was about to have an apoplectic fit, Elaine thought as she watched the surgeon's face turn red and heard him mutter an expletive under his breath. 'Just what I need!' he said. Not a word of concern for the accident victims, she thought angrily. Only concern for himself; for the fact that he would probably have to cancel at least part of his operating list. She flashed him a look of muted contempt. From somewhere she was finding the inner resources to deal with him.

The other doctors had turned to her in stunned silence. Tony Asher widened his eyes in a kind of pained horror. Then the voice came over the intercom: 'Attention, please. Attention, please. This is a general announcement for all operating room staff. There is a code purple in operation. Repeat...a code purple. Would all surgeons in the general surgery units and in the chest units, as well as all senior surgical residents in those units, report immediately to the emergency department and wait there for further instructions from Dr Claiborne. Please assemble in the main patient waiting-room. Would the on-call anaesthetists...the on-call anaesthetists only...report also to the emergency department immediately. Would all surgical interns remain in their units in the operating room. This announcement will be repeated.'

General pandemonium broke loose. Elaine rushed to her other three rooms where the nurses might not have heard the announcement, which had been in the corridors only. There was a chorus of, 'What's going on?'

'Prepare your room for a major abdominal case,'

Elaine said breathlessly to the nurses who stared at her wide-eyed, maintaining their calm. Most of them were preparing for such a case anyway. 'Get scrubbed so that we're ready for whatever cases we might get. I'll let you know as soon as I know myself.'

'Cathy,' she said tersely as she went back into Room 1, the room where Angie and Cathy were preparing for their first case, 'We need to get a chest tray; keep it on hand and set up another sterile table in case we have chest injuries that can't all be dealt with in the chest unit. I think we need to have at least one room set up for abdominal and chest combined. OK?'

'Sure! I was thinking of that. I'll get a tray,' Cathy said, going from the room quickly to get a sterile chest tray that would contain all the instruments they would need to open a chest.

'I'll get you some chest packs,' Elaine offered, grabbing a small, wheeled table on which to put the heavy packs, containing sterile drapes and sponges, for transportation back to the room from the storage area.

'How soon before we get the injured?' Angie said, looking frightened, yet managing to convey that she could cope with whatever came.

'Don't know yet. Not long, I should imagine. Our surgeons have all gone down to Emergency.'

'I'll get scrubbed,' Angie said, 'As soon as I've helped Cathy open up the chest packs.'

The telephone in the room shrilled again. It was Anne Temple.

'I've just had word,' she said, 'that there were a number of children on one of the buses and that we may have to take some of the overflow from Children's Hospital. If there are a lot of surgical cases they might not be able to cope with them all over there. Just wanted to let you know so that you've got the necessary paediatric anaesthetic equipment on hand.'

'Thank you for letting me know,' Elaine said, and hung up. They kept sets of paediatric equipment there, she knew, even though children were not often operated on in University Hospital and she racked her brains to think where they were kept as she hurried out of the room to go to the storage area.

'Hi,' Tony Asher hailed her. 'What gives?' The main corridor of the operating room was strangely empty now that there had been an exodus of the surgeons and anaesthetists who had been waiting to begin their first routine cases of the day.

'All I know,' she said, sidestepping another hurrying nurse, 'Is that we might get children and we might get chest injuries in this unit, as well as major abdominal. Maybe you should get scrubbed, Tony, to be ready. Once they've made the priority assessments in Emergency we'll be getting cases thick and fast, I should imagine.'

'Thank God I didn't drive this morning! There's a blizzard on. Looked like a white-out to me when I last got a chance to look out of a window.'

'Well, it's the right time of the year for it, Tony. Why are we all surprised when it comes, eh?'

'Denial, I expect. Yeah. . .well,' he sighed resignedly, 'I guess I'll get scrubbed. This is sure going to be a test of our disaster plan. Make sure you keep notes of all the things that go wrong; all the equipment. . . especially the vital equipment. . .that doesn't work, Elaine. And all the stuff that isn't where it's supposed to be. It'll be a real eye-opener.'

'Shut up, Tony,' she said. 'This is no time for your jokes.'

'I ain't joking, kid! Deadly serious! Maybe I'll go into psychiatry after this.' He put on his plastic goggles with an exaggerated flourish.

'Shut up anyway. Just get your hands under water.'

'OK. . .I'll scrub right now.'

'You do that. Then I'll know where you are.' She couldn't help grinning as he gave her a mock salute and clicked his heels together before turning on taps.

Telephones were ringing. People were either rushing about purposefully or standing poised, waiting for the first signs of definite action. Heads were poking round doors of the operating rooms or watching the double doors that led from the elevators, from where the stretchers bearing the first wave of the injured would be coming.

'How many major abdominal sets do we have in this place?' another nurse muttered to Elaine when they met in the stock room as she heaved a heavy tray of sterile instruments from a shelf and placed it on a wheeled table to push it back to her unit. 'I need a couple of chest sets too.'

'Enough for now, I should think.' Elaine smiled at her grimly in commiseration, eyeing what remained of their immediate stock. 'Maybe I'll get Pat to call the central supply unit anyway to order more packs. . .we're always running short of gown packs whenever there's an emergency.' As they talked they could hear announcements being repeated on the intercom and doctors being paged.

'Good idea,' the other nurse agreed. 'Better too many than not enough. Get them to give us all they've got on hand.'

'I will. Just leave a few for me, that's all!' she smiled, searching the shelves quickly for what she needed.

'Sure! Good luck!'

'Thanks. Same to you.' Elaine lifted down a heavy chest pack from a shelf, plus several others that they would need, wrapped in green sterile drapes. She quickly wheeled them back to her unit.

Patients who had been brought down to the operating

room for the first routine operations of the day were being wheeled back to another set of elevators by uniformed porters, leaving the emergency elevators clear. The patients looked resigned, peering around them to see where the excitement was, having had it explained to them that their own operations would have to be postponed, perhaps until the next day or Monday. Some of them looked around as though they were in a television play with themselves playing a starring role. 'Can't I stay here to watch?' one man joked as he was being wheeled away back to his floor.

'Afraid not,' the porter grinned.

Having distributed the packs and fetched a full set of paediatric anaesthetic equipment to keep on hand in the clean prep room of Room 1 in her unit, moving as fast as her legs would carry her without actually running, Elaine put a call through to Pat. Nothing ever fazed Pat, Elaine knew, as she punched in the number and thought of the receptionist who sat at the main desk just inside the operating room main doors. It was Pat, in partnership with the nursing co-ordinator, who kept the whole operating suite functioning efficiently.

'Pat,' she said, 'this is Elaine Stewart in Unit 2. Would you mind getting on to the CSU and ask them to send up all abdominal, gown and chest packs that they've got on hand. I guess they know there's a code purple on?'

'Yes, they do. I imagine they're just waiting for the word. I'll let them know,' Pat said.

'Thanks.' She replaced the receiver of the internal telephone in the clean prep room. All was quiet and orderly there; all packs and equipment piled up and arranged in sequence for what was to have been a full day of routine operations. Now all that equipment would be used for the emergencies as required.

She took the opportunity for a few quiet moments to

herself, taking several deep breaths and counting slowly up to ten with her eyes closed, willing herself to relax and to get ready mentally for the coming onslaught. More haste, less speed, she told herself. Just relax... take it easy. So far, so good.

They were as ready as they could be until they knew exactly what cases they would be getting. All they had to do now was check and re-check...then wait.

It started with another telephone call from the co-ordinator. 'Anne Temple here,' the voice said briskly. 'Got a paper and pen handy?'

'Yes,' Elaine said, the small pad of paper that she carried in her pocket ready in her hand, pen poised.

'Right! In Room 1 Dr Patterson, the chest surgeon, will be working with Dr Kenton on a woman who has a piece of metal fencing through her chest. One of the buses smashed into a chain-link fence at the side of the road, apparently, and bits of the fence came through the bus windows. By some miracle she's alive...and it seems to have missed her lung. It's gone through the side of her chest from front to back.'

'My God!' Elaine interjected.

'That's what I said. Anyway, they're going to open up her chest, pull the pipe out, clean up and assess the damage. According to the X-rays her lung on that side is OK; it still inflates...otherwise she might well have been dead by now. The emergency rescue guys at the accident scene managed to cut the pipe so that she has a few inches protruding from either side. It's on the right side and they think there might be a bit of liver damage too so Dr Kenton will be doing a laparotomy as soon as they've dealt with the chest...or they may decide to do the two procedures simultaneously.'

'Might Dr Kenton want to do a laparoscopy first?' Elaine ventured.

'Yes, he might well want to use a laparoscope to have a look-see before he does a laparotomy.'

'I'll have that ready,' she said.

Swallowing a nervous lump in her throat, Elaine somehow made further appropriate responses as her supervisor talked. This was sure going to be a test of her organisational skills and would show better than any reference what she was made of. Her mind raced over all the possibilities, deciding whether she had all the appropriate equipment on hand. Then a calmness came over her as it always did—a calculated, professional calmness.

'In Room 2,' Anne Temple was saying, 'Dr Alex White will be operating on a child, six years old, with a ruptured spleen and possibly damaged liver.'

'Oh, dear. . .'

'She's not too bad, actually, but they want to do her right away. In Room 3 internal abdominal injuries, a fractured femur and multiple superficial injuries from flying glass. Mike Richardson will be operating there. Room 4 the same, without the fracture. Dr Samuels will be operating there. Got all that?'

'Yes.' She scribbled frantically onto her pad of paper in her own kind of shorthand. 'We're all prepared, more or less,' she confirmed, 'apart from the laparoscopy stuff. . .'

'Good. I suggest you let your nurses know right away what they will be doing and then you go from room to room making sure they have all equipment required. That should keep you busy for a while. I want you to call me half an hour before you will be finishing a case so that I can schedule another case for your room—that should give you time to get ready.'

When the co-ordinator had hung up Elaine immediately dialled the orthopaedic unit. 'Janice?' she said, when the head nurse answered.

'Yeah. . .'

'Elaine here. Have you got a spare ortho set, with all the trimmings, for a fractured femur? I need it for my first case in one of my rooms, although they'll be doing the laparotomy first, I guess.'

'Yes, I have. You'll have to come and get it. . .I can't spare anyone. It's like Grand Central Station with a bomb scare on here!' Janice said.

Elaine laughed. 'I'll come myself as soon as I get a minute.'

'Right. It's in the clean prep room.'

It took only a few moments to run from room to room, telling the nurses what to expect. As she did so she saw stretchers coming down the corridor, most of them pushed by surgeons and anaesthetists walking at a brisk pace. Some were shouting instructions as they came within calling distance of their own rooms. Nurses were outside the rooms, waiting for them. Elaine recognised Claude Moreau and Matt; then there was Dr Samuels and Mike Richardson. . .then Alex White. In no time at all the response to the emergency had begun.

'I'll get you your ortho stuff after you've made a start. OK?' Elaine shouted into Room 3, holding the door open.

'OK,' the response came.

Then she was running to meet the first stretcher, pushed by the chest surgeon, Dr Patterson.

'Room 1,' she said to him, taking the end of the stretcher so that he could pull from the top end. The face of the woman who lay on it looked grey, her eyes closed. A clear plastic oxygen mask covered her nose and mouth.

'We decided to intubate her up here,' Dr Patterson said quietly to Elaine. 'She's breathing OK, amazingly.'

The patient's chest, with the piece of metal fence piping protruding from it, was partially exposed, her body padded and supported in such a way that the pipe would not be pushed further into her chest cavity. Elaine looked at it quickly, assessingly, before concentrating on manoeuvring the stretcher along the corridor which was filling up again with people. That was going to present a challenge to them, she thought soberly, to position the woman on the table so that further injury could be avoided. Two IV lines, connected to bags of fluid, ran into the woman's arms.

The circulating nurse in Room 1, Cathy, took over from her at the double doors to the room to help Dr Patterson with the stretcher, just as Claude Moreau joined them.

'I'll be giving the anaesthetic here, Cathy,' Dr Moreau said. 'I want to get her intubated right away— I'll need the flexible bronchoscope and the Xylocaine spray—before I actually give her the pentothal to put her under. OK?'

'Yes, everything's ready,' Cathy confirmed.

'Everything OK, Cath?' Elaine asked quietly.

'Yes, we'll be fine,' Cathy said.

'We'll need the laparoscopic equipment, Cath.'

'Yeah, I thought we would. I've been getting it together. . .I just need the video machine.'

'Right, I'll bring that for you.'

'She's being cross-matched right now,' Claude Moreau said to Elaine. 'Let me know as soon as the blood's ready and delivered.'

'OK,' she said.

Then she felt a touch on her arm and turned to see Raoul Kenton there, his face mask dangling around his neck. 'Where is the child being operated on?' he asked her. His face looked pale and unusually stiff with tension.

'Room 2,' she responded. 'Alex White will be there and Matt will be helping him.'

'I would like to operate on that child,' he said. 'I think there's more urgency there then we previously thought.'

The double doors to Room 1 closed behind Dr Patterson and she and Raoul were alone, as though isolated in the milling scene. The controlled chaos of the arriving accident victims was taking on a more frenetic pace as doctors and patients zeroed in on the rooms that were assigned to them and nurses ran to round up last-minute equipment.

Elaine frowned up at Raoul. 'You're in Room 1,' she said, 'assisting Dr Patterson.' Just to make sure she consulted her list again.

'Matt could assist him,' he said shortly. 'I would like to operate on that child.'

'This woman,' she said, her frown deepening, 'has a possible damaged liver. I don't think Dr Ferrera could deal with that.'

He took hold of her arm. 'Come with me,' he said.

'Where. . .?' In a few minutes he had marched with her to the prep room of Room 1.

'Are you telling me what to do?' he said tersely as he faced her once they were there, his face tight with anger.

Taken aback, she felt her mouth open in surprise. Why was he so up-tight all of a sudden? So unlike his usual calm self. 'Would it make any difference if I were Dr Kenton?' she asked reasonably, frowning. 'Dr Claiborne decided on the assignments. I had nothing to do with it.'

'That can be changed,' he replied shortly.

'Dr White was given the child because, as you know, he has had extensive paediatric experience. . .and the woman with the metal through her chest is the more urgent at the moment, so I was told.' As though to add authority to her words she again consulted her list, wondering momentarily whether she could have made a mistake.

'I know what Dr Claiborne wants,' he said. 'I prefer to operate on the child.'

Then Elaine felt her first, brief moment of something like panic. 'Wait here,' she said, stepping away from him, 'I'm going to speak to Dr White. I can't stand here arguing when there's so much to be done. . .when our patients are bleeding.' With that she fled from the room. What had got into him? Frantically she began to search for Dr White.

Dr Alex White was in the corridor outside Room 2 where he was to operate, bending over a stretcher on which a small child lay. With him was the anaesthetist. As Elaine came close to look at the child she instantly knew, with an intuitive sense of clarity, what Raoul's insistence was all about. The child, fine-boned, fair-haired and pale—a beautiful, frail child—was like his daughter, the girl in the photograph.

Transfixed, Elaine stood at the edge of the stretcher and stared down at the small face, with the eyes closed and the features in repose, long eyelashes fanning soft cheeks.

'She's not as bad as you might think,' Dr White murmured close to her ear, observing her expression, 'otherwise Children's Hospital would have taken her. There's a bit of intra-abdominal bleeding, probably from the spleen and maybe a bit from the liver. It's more of a slight ooze. . .nothing that we can't control quite easily, I think. She'll be OK.' Dr White was a thin, wiry man in his late thirties, a very intelligent, kind man.

'Dr White, I have a slight problem,' Elaine began, biting her lip uncertainly. 'I think I need your help.'

'Yes?' he said, his alert eyes on her face.

'Dr Kenton has told me that he wants to operate on

this girl. . .he more or less insists on it. . .whereas Dr
Claiborne expects him to help Dr Patterson. . .'

'The woman with the fence?'

'Yes. I. . .I'm not sure what to do with Dr Kenton. I
don't quite know how to put this. I have the feeling that
this is something personal with him. . .you know, his
daughter. . .'

'Where is Raoul?' he said decisively, seeming to
know exactly what she was talking about.

With a tremendous sense of relief Elaine explained
to him and watched him stride off purposefully. At the
same time she wanted to go to Raoul herself to say that
she understood. . .or thought she did. Time enough for
that a little later.

When the circulating nurse came out to be with the
child Elaine walked quickly to the orthopaedic unit to
get the sets of instruments that they required for the
fractured femur.

'Raoul wants to talk to you,' Dr White accosted her
as she returned with the packs and trays. 'He's waiting
for you in the same place.' He smiled at her, then said,
'Don't worry. I've sorted it out. . .for now.'

'Thanks, Dr White.' She returned his smile, gratitude
mingled with sorrow for Raoul in her glance and a fear
that perhaps he was cracking up at last. Perhaps he was
having a kind of delayed reaction; had reached some
point of no return, against which his carefully built
defences were inadequate.

Having left the orthopaedic instruments in Room 3,
she hurried to the Room 1 prep room, her heart in her
mouth, fearful of what she might find.

'I want to apologise.' Raoul was the first to speak as
soon as she entered the cramped room. 'I had no right
to put you on the spot like that. Of course, it is up to
Dr Claiborne to decide. Are they ready for me yet in
Room 1?' The pallor and tension on his face and his

haunted eyes made her heart contract with anguish.

'They will be in about ten minutes,' she whispered. 'It's going to take them time to get the patient positioned properly on the operating table...and they want to put her under the anaesthetic first, of course.'

'Yes, of course. I'll be there,' he said. 'Thank you, Elaine...for being so understanding. I'm not sure what got into me just then...a mental aberration. Dr Claiborne was right.'

Instinctively, putting all reticence aside, she went up to him and put her hands on his shoulders. 'She's not your daughter, Raoul,' she said gently. 'Dr White is very capable; he isn't going to let her die. She isn't really very badly injured, so he said...and she's going to be all right. I'll keep you informed of what goes on in that room.'

A spasm of pain seemed to cross his attractive face; his lips twisted in a second or two of private anguish as his eyes appeared not to focus on her but to see something else entirely. Impulsively she put her arms around his neck, drawing him to her, then put her lips gently on his. Trembling, she was overwhelmed by his anguish and her own longing.

For a few seconds their lips made contact and then he pulled her into his arms roughly with a hoarse groan and was crushing her to him, his mouth grinding into hers with a desperate, hungry need, and she matched him with her response.

What seemed like minutes were only seconds as they clung and then pulled apart. They were needed elsewhere. Raoul gripped her arm at the same time that he pulled back. 'You once offered to listen while I talked,' he said, a wild look of grief in his eyes. 'Is that offer still open?'

'Yes,' she whispered. 'Yes...it always will be, Raoul. If you want to talk, make it soon.' Impulsively she reached up to touch his face. 'I'll be ready when you are. And we have to go to work now.'

'Tonight?' he asked intensely. 'When all this is over? Come to my house. Please.'

'Yes. . .yes, I will.' Taking both his hands in his, she squeezed them hard, 'They're waiting for you in Room 1.' Standing on tiptoe, she kissed him quickly on the cheek and left the room.

With no time to reflect on what had happened between them, she paused only long enough to tie on her mask before she plunged into the mad work scene, knowing that she would be all right. So would Raoul be all right, she knew that with certainty. And, more importantly, so would their patient, whom they were rapidly coming to think of as 'the woman with the fence'. It was time to find out her name.

What she did know for sure was that that woman had two of the best surgeons in University Hospital—no, in the whole of Gresham—working on her. And one of the best anaesthetists.

The odds against ever getting a piece of fence through your chest in a lifetime were very great. Elaine Stewart, she told herself proudly and with determination as she entered Room 1, With this team the odds of survival for that woman are very high indeed.

CHAPTER THIRTEEN

'SHE's all right. . .the little girl, Dr Kenton. They just took her out to the recovery room.'

The expression in Dr Kenton's eyes was hard to see as he raised his head from what he was doing at the operating table to nod an acknowledgement of her whispered information, his eyes being covered with the ubiquitous goggles.

During her duties of supervising the four rooms in her unit Elaine had kept a close eye on the operation in Room 2 with Dr White. She had made sure that she was there when the girl had come round from the anaesthetic afterwards and had been wheeled out of the room. Dr White had told her that the mother was waiting and that she would be allowed into the recovery room to see her daughter.

In Room 1 they had first of all done a laparoscopy on the woman. A tiny incision had been made into her abdominal cavity with a thin, metal scope, which enabled the cavity to be illuminated and the soft organs to show up on a video screen. They had discovered that the bleeding was minimal, yet they would have to open up the abdominal cavity later in order to get it stopped. The chest was the first priority.

'Would you like to go for a coffee-break, Cathy?' Elaine offered. 'This seems like as good a time as any.' The metal pipe in the patient's chest had been removed and now the chest cavity was being irrigated and minor abrasions dealt with. Antibiotics were being given with the intravenous fluid.

'I sure would,' Cathy said. 'Then you ought to go,

Elaine. I'll cover for you. What's happening next door in Room 2, now that they've finished the child?'

'Another laparoscopy, repair of multiple lacerations and a possible below-knee amputation. By the look of the patient every window in that bus must have smashed. It's really awful. They've got the plastic surgeons working on him,' Elaine said, recalling the bloody face of their patient that had been hit by flying glass. 'He's got bits of glass stuck in his face...it's going to take them hours to pick it all out. His eyes are OK, thank God.'

Cathy let out an involuntary sigh. 'I can't wait to go on vacation,' she said. 'I'm going off to Florida in two weeks' time. Just the vision of those palm trees, that azure sea, helps me to keep sane.'

Cathy slipped out of the room and Elaine took over her duties, making sure that the paperwork of the operating procedure was up to date and ensuring that the scrub nurse, Angie, had the sponges, sutures and other supplies that she needed and that Dr Moreau had the bags of blood for transfusion, as well as other IV fluids, that he needed for their patient.

She looked at the monitors that displayed the patient's vital signs. So far, although progress was painstaking and slow, all was well. There was a quiet peace in the room, engendered by a dedicated purpose. It was going to be a long, hectic day. She knew beyond doubt that she would not get a lunch break and that she had better make the most of whatever coffee-break she could get; that they would all be working overtime well into the evening. They would do it willingly; it was all part of the job.

'What was it like down in Emergency earlier on?' She spoke quietly to Claude Moreau as he sat at the head of the operating table next to the anaesthetic machine that delivered the gases to keep their patient unconscious. 'I was wondering whether we shall get around to doing any of our scheduled patients later on today.'

'Possibly we'll get one or two done... Depends on how many of our emergency laparoscope patients turn into full-scale laparotomies,' Dr Moreau said thoughtfully, fixing his pale blue glance on her. 'It was a bit like a battle zone down there at one point. Almost all the people on those buses had superficial, multiple cuts from glass. Fortunately many of those look far worse at first glance than they turn out to be...they bleed like crazy.'

It was well after six o'clock in the evening when it all came to an end.

'There's no way that the evening staff can clear up this mess so we'd better get stuck in,' Elaine said to Angie as the last patient was wheeled out of Room 1 and she stood with hands on hips, surveying the chaos that was left behind. 'I've already resigned myself to coming in tomorrow to get things back in order.'

'That's the price you pay for being head nurse,' Angie commented wearily. 'You have to come in on weekends.'

'Hi there, girls!' Matt's cheery voice hailed them from the doorway. 'You look about as whacked as I feel. How about coming over to the bar for a drink later...all of you?' Matt had spent most of the day going from room to room, wherever he was needed the most.

'Not tonight, Matt, thanks,' Angie said. 'I haven't got the energy to put one foot in front of the other; it's going to take all my energy just to get home in this weather. I think I'm just going to call a taxi and let someone else worry about the roads...so long as I don't have to push the damn thing.'

'Elaine?'

'No, thanks, Matt. I just want to get home after all this clearing up,' she said, pulling off her cap, running her fingers through her short hair so that it stood on end and ripping off her face mask.

'Don't worry, *cara*,' Matt said teasingly, 'when we're married I'll take you away from all this.'

Elaine shot him an irritated glance, not knowing what he was playing at. Several times over the last few days he had dropped hints that there was more between them than there actually was and some of those remarks had been within Raoul's hearing. . .almost as though Matt wanted to provoke something.

'What makes you think she wants to be taken away from all this?' Cathy said drily, pausing in her task of turning off the nitrous oxide and oxygen supply to the anaesthetic machine. 'And with you, of all people?'

'He thinks he's irresistible,' Angie laughed, just as Raoul and Claude Moreau came back into the room.

They had both removed their head-gear and both looked exhausted. Raoul shot Elaine a quick glance, silently reminding her of their arrangement,

'Ah. . .you've done part of my job for me, Miss Stravinsky,' Dr Moreau said to Cathy. 'Thank you. I usually try to turn off the gases and clear up at least a bit of my mess before I go. I just wanted to check our last patient in the recovery room first.'

Cathy flushed with pleasure, her thin, serious face lighting up, and Elaine wondered whether Claude Moreau had any idea of how devoted Cathy was to him. Being a very perceptive man, he must have some idea, she decided, even though Cathy never let her personal feelings interfere with her work.

Raoul's presence sent a frisson of awareness through her when he came to stand near her. 'Seven-fifteen OK?' he said to her as Cathy and Dr Moreau were talking, diverting attention. There had been a terrible fear in her that he would not follow through with his intention to talk to her.

Suddenly, standing there with him, surrounded by the chaos and debris of an absolutely crazy day and sharing the professional accomplishment, she finally admitted to herself that she loved Raoul Kenton. . .was not just attracted to him physically. And with equal conviction she decided that she didn't care who knew it. . .or who knew that they were going to spend time together that evening at his house.

The whole world could know for all she cared, she thought with exhilaration as he looked at her. Yes, it was true that he devoured her with his eyes, she realised. She liked it. . .she liked everything about him.

'Yes, that's fine,' she agreed breathlessly, her eyes shining. 'Where?'

'The Fraser lobby.' He smiled at her, a slow smile of recognition.

She nodded again, returning his smile, aware that both Matt and Angie were looking at them.

There had been little conversation during the drive to Raoul's house through heavy snow.

Not only were they both exhausted, they were both preoccupied with mental images of all that they had seen that day: images of bloody faces; images of ruptured spleens and lacerated livers, showing up in brilliant colour on video screens; images of horrendous chest injuries, head injuries, fractures. . .

On the way home he had stopped to buy wine and food, instructing her to wait in the car.

Now she sat on a sofa beside a roaring fire, holding a glass of that wine. It glowed ruby red in the firelight, the only light in the cosy sitting-room of his house where they had also eaten a supper prepared by him. He had refused any help from her, telling her to rest.

'That was absolutely wonderful. . .thank you,' she said, looking up at him, from where she sat with her legs tucked under her as he stood in front of her. Clad in the jeans and casual sweater that she had worn to work that day, she felt cosy yet a little self-conscious in his beautiful home, even though the house itself looked very lived-in. The debris of their supper was on the table behind them. 'Could I do anything?'

'No. . .I thought I'd make coffee later,' he said, reaching forward to take the wine glass out of her hand. He too wore jeans, and a casual striped shirt, open at the neck.

Already his beeper had gone off several times during the meal; the telephone had called him away also. Yet somehow he had managed not to leave her. 'Fate must be on our side,' he murmured, smiling. 'Peace reigns at last.'

Warmed and relaxed by the wine though she was, Elaine felt a familiar tension creep over her again as he lowered himself onto the small rug in front of the fire and sat there with his hands between his raised knees, simply looking at her, engaging her attention as though challenging her to look away. She could not look away.

If he had asked her then to go to bed with him she would have unfolded herself from the sofa and gone with him up the dark, sweeping staircase of the lovely old house that she had seen briefly as they had come in. Indeed, there was a longing in her to see where he slept in his own home, away from the impersonal place where he sometimes slept when on call. The whole place was comfortable and beautiful in an unostentatious way. . .like him, she thought.

'Was this where you lived with your wife and daughter?' Not taking her eyes from his, she articulated the question deliberately—it had to be asked. No doubt he could read the commiseration that she felt was clearly on her face. . .and the love.

'No. . .' he said.

'Why have you taken away my wine?' she whispered. 'With you I think I need wine.' The smile on her lips, softening her words, found an answering smile in him and she found her heart responding to his physical presence, betraying her need of him. There was no sound in the room other than the crackling of the fire and the muted ticking of an old clock in the hallway.

'I need you sober, without your judgement clouded by alcohol,' he said, the slow smile he was giving her lighting his face and his eyes. 'Afterwards you can have a whole bottle of wine to yourself, if you wish.' That smile, curving his sensual mouth, became the focus of her attention.

'Are you ready to talk now?' she asked softly. 'Because if you are. . .I'm as ready to listen as I'll ever be.'

Slowly, without breaking the mesmerising eye contact, he held out a hand to her and she found herself uncoiling as though in slow motion, reaching forward to take his hand and responding to the pressure of it as he pulled her down beside him on the rug. The flames of the firelight flickered over them with red fingers; the welcome heat warmed her body.

They lay side by side, she the furthest away from the fire, his leg pressed against hers and their hands still touching as though by accident. The contact started an inner trembling in her, a slow, inevitable sensitisation to his presence, and she closed her eyes.

Perhaps, after all, she couldn't deal with this; couldn't deal with him. He had vowed not to make love to her again yet she had made no such vow; would not have the power to prevent herself. . .

'Lift your head up,' he murmured. When she opened

her eyes he had a cushion to place under her head and one for himself too.

As he leaned over her he stilled, did not move away, and she put her arms around his neck. 'Raoul. . .' She said his name softly.

With a deep intake of breath, let out on a sigh, he supported himself on his elbows either side of her face. Slowly, deliberately, he lowered himself to kiss her. As she focussed on his mouth her lips parted to receive him. 'Oh. . . God. . . Elaine.' His murmured words were barely audible. 'My love. . .my darling.'

Don't say that! she protested silently. Don't say that unless you mean it. . .

Then her hands were in his thick hair, caressing, glorying in the feel of him. Her whole body felt alive as she breathed in the faint scent of a rare cologne, his face so close to hers. Then his lips were on hers, softly, like the touch of a butterfly's wing as he teased her; touching, then moving away again, teasing her lips. Gradually the contact deepened and held longer as she gave a small, helpless moan of longing, sensing in him the desire and excitement that matched her own.

They both tasted of the rich, full-bodied wine. 'Mmm. . .' His deep-throated murmur of appreciation sparked a wave of desire through her that was like an exquisite physical touch.

'I. . .need that wine, Raoul,' she said.

'Here. . .' he murmured unevenly, breaking contact for a moment, his breathing ragged and fast like her own. He held her glass of wine to her mouth so that she sipped from it, wetting her lips while he supported her head.

'Mmm. . .I should have thought of this before I took your glass away. . .' His voice was soft with laughter, husky with desire, as between words he tasted the wine that was on her lips.

Again and again she sipped and he made intimate contact with her mouth until she, her eyes closed weakly with desire, was compliant in his arms, leaning against him. With his mouth on hers he supported her weight with one arm.

Then they both began to laugh helplessly after he said regretfully, 'It's all gone!' The cares, the responsibility and the horror of the day receded a little for them.

Leaning together breathlessly, they looked at each other. 'Shall I open another bottle?' he offered.

'I. . .I'm afraid I really would be drunk,' she stammered slightly, consumed by her newly admitted love. 'Then I. . .I wouldn't be able to listen to you. And you must talk, Raoul. . .you must.'

'I know,' he agreed. 'It's just that you're so delectable, little Miss Stewart. I'm having trouble resisting.'

'You said it wouldn't happen again,' she reminded him.

'I know. . . I've said a lot of stupid things.' His voice was persuasive against her ear, 'Would you like it to happen again?'

'Yes. . .you know I would,' she admitted honestly. 'I also remember how you rejected me, Raoul. I. . .I was very hurt.'

If they went to bed then, if they indulged in the explosive love-making from which they hovered just on the brink, if she gave in to the ecstasy that she knew was waiting for her with him—perhaps he would never talk. Perhaps the moment would never be right again as she felt it was right now.

'Talk,' she said, looking into his eyes that were almost black, the pupils large and dark, knowing that hers were the same. . .the tell-tale mark of sexual desire. 'Raoul. . .you must talk. That's what we came for.'

He hugged her to him then, rocking her back and forth in his strong arms. She felt wanted and loved. . . .

yes, loved, she thought with surprise. Yet he had never said that he loved her. As she responded blindly, holding him in turn, she decided that she didn't care what it all meant.

'I didn't reject you,' he said.

'Yes, you did,' she countered.

The clock in the hallway struck the hour. Absently she counted the strokes, to ten. 'It's ten o'clock,' she said, amazed at how the night was going by. Time had lost all significance.

'You don't say,' he said indulgently, laughing at her. 'What happens at ten o'clock?'

'I was wondering if you might turn into a frog,' she said facetiously.

'That happens at midnight if you'll stay that long. . . please. Sometimes I think you believe I'm one already,' he said.

'No, I don't.' With determination and a terrible regret she moved out of his arms to lie back on the rug, wriggling to make herself comfortable and aware that he watched every movement she made. 'Raoul. . .what happened today? I want to know. What did you feel when you first saw that little girl in the emergency department. . .that little fair girl who looks so much like your daughter? Tell me. . .please.'

After he had lowered himself beside her he was silent for such a long time that she thought he had decided against confiding in her. Wisely she let the silence stretch as she gradually sensed the tension of waiting in him—a searching for the right words. When he started to talk his voice sounded different, as though rusty from disuse.

'My wife, Jane, couldn't accept that neither I nor anyone else could save our daughter. It was as though she, Jane, made me personally responsible for her death. . .while I was in utter hell myself, of course.

Everything that could possibly have been done for her was done. . .medically.' The voice slowed to a halt, husky with pain.

'What was your daughter's name?' Elaine ventured, feeling something of the depth of his grief.

'Samantha. We called her Sammy.' The word 'we', an exclusive word, hung uncomfortably between them. She did not intrude.

'Go on,' she commanded simply.

'I threw myself into work. . .after Sammy died; helping other people was somehow a compensation for me—for the fact that I could not, ultimately, help my daughter. That was my response. Jane's was quite the opposite. . . She withdrew from the world, like a wild animal hides away when it's hurt.' He was speaking carefully, recalling, thinking it all out. 'Working so much did not exactly help my marriage although it was pretty much over by then anyway.'

When he moved slightly next to her, his hand inadvertently touched hers and she grasped it, holding it tightly, feeling a knot of emotion rise in her throat. He did not pull away but returned the pressure convulsively.

'I can't pretend that I didn't love my wife,' he said, 'because that would be a lie. I did love her. We grew apart irrevocably after the death of our daughter. Our ways of coping seemed mutually exclusive. Ultimately we had nothing to give each other because we were both suffering too much.'

'And now. . .what do you feel? And where is she?'

'She's with someone else, as happy as I think she'll ever be. We can't stand the sight of each other now because all we remember is the pain. When I saw that child today it all came back. . .the helplessness of it. That's why I wanted to operate. . .to do something.' His voice was bleak with mourning.

'Yes, I understand,' she whispered. 'That's what I thought at the time.'

As though the floodgates of emotion had at long last opened he talked on, his voice husky, while she listened. From time to time they were aware of the clock striking the half-hour and the hour. When at last he fell silent the clock struck one. . .one o'clock in the morning.

Feeling stiff from not having moved and tense with the effort of suppressing tears of empathy, Elaine struggled to her feet to put a log on the fire that had died down to glowing embers. Then, going to the French doors that overlooked the back garden, she pulled aside the heavy drapes. Snow was banked up, several feet high, against the glass and thick flakes swirled against it. She gasped, 'Look! Raoul. . .the amount of snow!'

Raoul got to his feet and came to stand behind her, putting his hands on her shoulders and pulling her back to rest against him as they looked out.

'The world has moved on since we've been talking,' she said, leaning her head sideways against his chest.

'That could be a metaphor for my life over the past few years,' he murmured, his lips touching her hair. Slowly she turned round to face him so that she was in the circle of his arms. Firelight danced on her face as she looked up at him shyly: the look told him that she would never take him for granted.

'You know you said once that you wouldn't want to work with someone who couldn't cry?' she said. 'Well, I wouldn't either. There's already too much indifference in the world. I. . .I'm glad you reacted the way you did today. It means you're human.'

'After all?' he teased. 'So I'm not going to turn into a frog?'

She laughed, putting her arms around him. 'No, I won't let you.'

'Because you've broken the spell? Hmm? Like a fairy tale.' He kissed her on the mouth and she gave herself up to him, daring to hope that there could be something between them.

'I think we're snowed in,' she ventured, turning to look at the falling snow that was making little tapping noises against the glass.

'You'll have to stay with me now,' he said huskily, holding her close.

'Looks like it,' she said.

'And I don't mean just for tonight... Look at me, Elaine...love.'

Slowly she tilted back her head to look at him, knowing that all the love and longing that she felt for him, all that she hoped for them both, was in her big, haunted, grey eyes.

'So fragile...and yet so strong,' he murmured, taking her face into his hands as though she were a child. 'Little Miss Stewart. Stay with me. Will you?'

'Yes...' There was no other answer that she could give; there never had been. 'I love you, Raoul...so much. I tried not to...'

'I tried not to as well...like trying to hold back the tide. I love you, you funny, sweet, adorable little Miss Stewart. I knew you were trouble as soon as I clapped eyes on you,' he said, holding her to him as though he wanted to hold her for ever, the warmth of relief lightening his voice. 'I want to sleep with you; I want to hear you say that you love me, over and over again...that we can make a life together.'

'Your wishes shall be granted, oh Prince,' she murmured huskily, teasing him, willing away his demons. 'I'm ready.'

Then his firm mouth was on hers, taking her and

giving himself also. . .she realised then, with a wild surge of joy. Somehow, between them, they had managed to overcome the past—to start again. Somehow there had been a healing touch and it had come with her help. He had accepted.

SINGLE LETTER SWITCH

A year's supply of Mills & Boon Presents™ novels— absolutely FREE!

Would you like to win a year's supply of passionate compelling and provocative romances? Well, you can and the're free! Simply complete the grid below and send it to us by 31st May 1997. The first five correct entries picked after the closing date will win a year's supply of Mills & Boon Presents™ novels (six books every month—worth over £150). What could be easier?

S	T	O	C	K
P	L	A	T	E

Clues:

A   To pile up
B   To ease off or a reduction
C   A dark colour
D   Empty or missing
E   A piece of wood
F   Common abbreviation for an aircraft

Please turn over for details of how to enter ☞

How to enter...

There are two five letter words provided in the grid overleaf. The first one being STOCK the other PLATE. All you have to do is write down the words that are missing by changing just one letter at a time to form a new word and eventually change the word STOCK into PLATE. You only have eight chances but we have supplied you with clues as to what each one is. Good Luck!

When you have completed the grid don't forget to fill in your name and address in the space provided below and pop this page into an envelope (you don't even need a stamp) and post it today. Hurry—competition ends 31st May 1997.

Mills & Boon® Single Letter Switch
FREEPOST
Croydon
Surrey
CR9 3WZ

Are you a Reader Service Subscriber?   Yes ❑   No ❑

Ms/Mrs/Miss/Mr _____

Address _____

_____

_____ Postcode _____

One application per household.

You may be mailed with other offers from other reputable companies as a result of this application. If you would prefer not to receive such offers, please tick box.   ❑

C6K